DECLAN

LARAMIE BRISCOE

Editing: Katy Nielson

Cover Design: LB Design

Photography: Wander Aguiar

Cover Model: Brooke

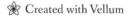 Created with Vellum

NEW RELEASE ALERTS

JOIN MY MAILING LIST
http://sitel.ink/LBList

JOIN MY READERS GROUP
fbl.ink/LaramiesLounge

TEXT LARAMIE TO 88202

BLURB

My sister's best friend has always taken my breath away...

Declan Tennyson

At twenty-two, most guys my age are living it up; swiping left and right, trying to find what's good for the night instead of what's good for life.

Me? With my dad looking to slow down to spend more time with my mom after twenty plus years of love, I'm left with a life impacting decision to make.

Take the shop – or make my own way.

I thought I had it all worked out, until a single mom with brunette hair, blue eyes, and the cutest son ever needed my help on a freezing, snowy night.

Claudia Wilson

Declan Tennyson was cute and annoying. My best friend's little brother could always be counted on to be underfoot or secretly listening to our girl talk.

But in the last three years?

He grew into a man without me noticing.

Being a single mom is harder than I ever expected it to be, and I haven't had time to notice anything.

Not until the night Declan saved us in the snow, and if I'm not careful, he's gonna end up saving me from myself.

CHAPTER 1
DECLAN

THE NIGHT SKY sparkles in the inky blackness as the snow crunches under my boots. The city is asleep, partly because of the late hour, and partly because the weather has been shit which is why I'm walking home from the bar tonight and not driving my truck.

Stuffing my hands into the pockets of my jacket and ducking my head into the wind, I pick up the pace. I stayed out longer than I meant to, and my morning wake-up call is going to come in just a few hours.

Pulling my phone out of my back pocket, I check the temperature.

Fifteen degrees.

My face is about to freeze off. Luckily, I only have a few more blocks to go.

"How am I going to get us out of this mess?"

The voice of a woman cuts through the night. It's one of distress and irritation. It's also one that sounds familiar to me. Picking up my speed, I hurry to where I heard the sound coming from.

Once I turn the corner, I see a little Toyota I recognize. A brunette is standing beside it with her hands held on top of her head; one I've always thought was beautiful. One who has been the star of so many of my adolescent fantasies. I haven't seen her as much in the last couple of years, not since she became a single mother and stopped hanging out with my sister, Riley, so much.

"Claudia?" I call out, not believing what I'm seeing.

"Declan." The relief is palpable. "Did I conjure you up?"

Chuckling, I hurry over to where she stands. "No, I'm coming from the bar up the street. I decided to walk since the roads are shit, and you know, I didn't think driving my bike would be a safe bet."

She blows out a breath. "I should've done the same, but I couldn't with him." She points into the backseat.

"How's the little guy?" I look in, noticing he's knocked out, his head jacked to the side against his car seat.

"He's good," she smiles softly. "He's slept through this whole situation." She holds her hands out in front of her, as if she's saying she can't imagine how.

"What's going on here?"

She sighs heavily. "I'm supposed to be on my shift at the hospital right now, but I got stuck as you can see. I called his dad to see if he could come help us," she stops talking and seems to be fighting tears. "He said he'd be here, but that was three hours ago, and I've just gotten stuck worse."

"Claud, I'm sorry."

"It's okay," she sniffs. "It is what it is."

"Let's see if we can get you out."

I walk around the car, trying to figure out the best way to get her out of the embankment she's gotten herself stuck in.

"What do you want me to do?" she asks.

"Get back in the car. I'm gonna push." I give a testing push on the bumper. "Roll down your window so you can hear me."

"Thank you so much, Declan," she says before getting into the driver's seat.

"Not a problem, and don't thank me until I get you outta here."

I rock the car back and forth, trying to get it out of the hole she's dug herself into by continuing to spin the wheels.

"Turn it to the left and give it some gas," I instruct.

She does as I've told her and I take a little bit of a running start to get some force behind my push. It starts to move. My footing begins to slip but I continue pushing. "Gas, gas, gas... don't be scared."

Claudia continues. I'm proud she doesn't take it easy. I can remember the first time I got myself stuck in the snow and ice. It'd been hard to trust I was doing the right thing.

"Now, crank it to the right slightly. Okay, back to the left and gas, gas, gas."

"Yay!" she yells as she gets back onto the road. The brine and sand allow her tires to grip the surface, although it's still slick.

Since it's just the two of us on the road, she gets out and comes around, throwing her arms around my neck. "Thank you so much. Guess all those afternoons of you and your friends riding bikes in your backyard in the mud, paid off. All those times you got stuck ended up being a life skill, huh?"

The hug takes me by surprise. She hasn't hugged me since before I hit puberty, and this time I can't help but notice the feel of her chest against mine.

"I forgot about riding my bike in the mud when I was a kid. I always loved getting you and Riley dirty, though. It was my favorite to send you and two upstairs crying because I'd gotten your clothes dirty. Luckily for you, I've grown up since then. Are you still going to work?"

"Yeah." Her eyes don't meet mine. "I can't afford to lose the hours. Even though I'm late, I'll still be able to get paid for something."

"Do you feel comfortable driving yourself?" I eye the ice and snow-covered asphalt.

"We'll just take it slow," she shrugs, running her hands up and down her arms.

But I can tell by the way her lips tremble she isn't comfortable, she's just used to taking care of things on her own. Of pushing aside her needs and fears, and doing what needs to be done.

Mind made up, I grab her hand, ignoring how good it feels. Walking her over to the passenger side, I open the door. "Get in. I'll take him wherever it was you were taking him and then we'll swing you by work. Just let me know what time you get off and I'll make sure to be there."

"No," she protests. "We're not your responsibility."

"Maybe not, but I think we both know Riley would have my ass if she knew I left you alone in this vulnerable situation."

She makes a noise in the back of her throat. "She would definitely have a few choice words to say."

Raising an eyebrow, I look at her, thinking about the mouth on my sister. She could make a sailor blush on the right night. "A few?"

She wrinkles her nose, seeming to think about Riley and how she'd react. "Alright, Declan, thank you. We appreciate it."

After getting into the driver's seat, I buckle in and then ease onto the street, aware of the precious cargo I'm transporting.

CHAPTER 2
CLAUDIA

WHEN I GLANCE over at Declan, it's like I'm seeing him for the first time. I've known him for years. Riley's my best friend, for goodness' sake. She and I started hanging out the year she moved to the neighborhood. I've been around his entire life, but I've never looked at him like I am right now.

"You shouldn't even be out in this mess," he whistles through his teeth.

My gaze is glued to where his gloveless hands grip the steering wheel. It's not as if I've never seen his tattoos before, but I can't remember a time when they've caught my attention as much as they are right now. I've seen him without a shirt but, at this moment, those hands are the sexiest things I've witnessed – which either says a lot about him or about me. Pulling back to the moment, I respond to his previous words.

"I wish I didn't have to be," I sigh. "I hate working this shift, but I get a shift differential. It's three bucks more an hour."

"What happens with him?" He tilts his head to where Jay is asleep in his car seat.

"Luckily, they have childcare. I get off at seven in the morning and my

mom or Riley will take him for a few hours for me. It seems wrong to put him in daycare day and night, ya know? Although he mostly sleeps when I'm at work, I don't want him to always have people he doesn't know watching him." I shrug.

"You don't get much sleep, do you?" Declan barely puts on the brakes so we can come to a stop at a red light.

I laugh, shaking my head. "Not at all. I dream of the sleep I used to get when I do. Every once in a while, I use one of the empty rooms to get a nap when we aren't super busy. One of my co-workers looks out for me when I do."

"Does Jay's dad ever help? I don't remember him much."

"Neither does Jay, and no, he doesn't help. You saw what a joke it was for him to say he'd come to help me get out of the mess I was in with the car. That's what he does all the time, makes promises and never keeps them. He's supposed to pay child support. He did it twice and now he's so far behind that if he gets pulled over or a police officer runs his name, he'll go to jail. I don't hope he'll ever catch up or want to see Jay." I don't admit this to many people, but I can trust Declan. I must be careful because I did the same thing with Jay's dad. I'm the type of person who wants to see the good in others. It gets me in trouble more often than not.

"That's tough. I'm sorry," he mumbles.

"No, I'm sorry. You probably asked to be polite and I just unloaded all my irritation at another man on you." Now I'm an asshole to a guy who wanted to help us. It's rare someone asks me how things are going and includes Jay in the equation. My face flames with the embarrassment of letting my mouth speak more than it should have. Sweat beads on my forehead as I think about what I've said to Declan. I wish the passenger seat would open up and swallow me into a dark hole.

We pull up to the hospital and he parks. Fumbling with my seatbelt, I'm trying to get out of this car as quickly as possible.

"Hey." He reaches over, grabbing hold of my shaking hand to stop my motion. "I don't do anything to be polite."

Lifting my eyes, I catch the slight tilt of his lips. "Are you teasing me?"

"No, I'm being honest. If there's one thing I've learned working at the shop with Dad and his manager, G, is you can't be polite in that sense. If you do, you'll listen to people's sob stories and give them free service for the rest of their natural-born lives. I wouldn't have asked if I didn't want to know."

Rolling my lips together, I give him a small smile. "Thank you."

"There's no reason for you to thank me. There's absolutely no way I would've let the two of you be out in this by your-selves. What time do you get off work?"

My mind is blank as I try to figure out why he's asking. "I should get off at six a.m., but I wanna try and make up as much time as possible, so I'm going to push for eight. Why?"

"While I don't mind hoofing it home from here, I do mind you driving him home in this." He jerks his finger behind him to where Jay is still asleep in his car seat. "I'll be awake at five. I have to get things going for the shop anyway. You get off at six, let me know. You get off at eight, let me know. Either way, I'll be here."

Guilt washes over me, suffocating like a blanket. Since it's been Jay and me, I've had a lot of that.

Guilt.

It comes in different shapes and sizes and in waves. It's fluc-tuating, a living and breathing thing. I never know what might trigger it. It could be that I have him out in the middle of a snowstorm or that he has no dad to go to the father/son activi-ties with at daycare. On the same token, it could be when I have to choose between a toy he wants or our electric bill. Working overtime so that I can give him both or put a little back into savings all weigh on me.

And that's just anything that has to do with Jay. Forget when I'm asking my mom to watch him on her day off so I can get a few things done, or when I'm forced to leave him with a babysitter he doesn't know.

Now I'm bringing my best friend's brother into it; a kid who has no worries in the world.

"I can't ask you to do that," I say with a shake of my head.

"You're not asking me, I'm insisting. Actually, I'm demanding. Not only will I lose respect for myself, but I'll also hear about it from Riley, my mom, and dad."

"Dec..."

The hand on mine reaches up until it gets to my chin. His thumb tilts my chin upward and back. His serious blue eyes meet mine. "What did I say to you? I don't do anything to be polite. You call me. While some people don't want the responsibility, I'm not one of them. If you need help, I'm the one who'll give it to you."

CHAPTER 3
DECLAN

I'M EXHAUSTED as I trudge up the steps to my apartment. A few years ago, Dad bought two more buildings on the same block so he could expand the shop. Each of those buildings has their own apartment on the top level, meaning Riley and I were able to move out, but still stay close. I'm going up the back way because I don't want the cameras to go off, letting my dad know I've been out all night. Although I'm of age, both he and Mom still worry.

Judging by the amount of snow on the steps and landing, I'll be shoveling before I do anything else. When I finally get upstairs and open the door, I'm greeted by the heat I left on. When I was growing up, Mom was going through menopause, and at some point, it became a running joke in our house that she couldn't take off anymore clothes, but we could put them on. So many winter nights, my dad and I froze our asses off in the name of his love for her. I promised myself I wouldn't do the same when I moved out. I will sweat and go down to shorts with no shirt before I cut the heat down, just out of principle.

I'm slipping my jacket off when there's a knock at my door.

Who the fuck is it at this time of night, or morning? When I open the door, I roll my eyes heavenward. "I already have a mom. I don't need a second one."

My sister *tsks* as she walks in. "What the hell are you doing coming in so late?"

"Not that I owe you any explanation since I'm a grown-ass man, but I was helping your BFF."

She wrinkles her nose. "Why were you helping Claudia?"

I'm starving, so while we're talking, I go about making myself a quick sandwich to eat. "I went to the bar tonight."

She interrupts, snorting unapologetically. "Only you would go to the bar in the middle of a fucking blizzard."

"I was bored," I shrug. "Not all of us have the most perfect partner in the world. Some of us get lonely. Anyway, I was walking back because no way would I be driving in any of this bullshit, and she and Jay were stuck in an embankment. She was scared to give it enough gas to get out of there. I stopped and helped her."

Riley smirks. "I wouldn't say I have the most perfect partner. He's just around whenever I need a little pick me up, without all the messy feelings. So my question is did you stop to help her because she's my best friend, or because you're a Good Samaritan?"

"First of all, feelings aren't messy, and does it really matter?" I ask around the bread in my mouth.

"Yes," she grins. "You're a nice guy, but you hardly ever let anyone know that about you. If you stopped to help her, then you must care. Otherwise you probably would've called Triple A and waited for someone else to do the job."

She's tried to get me to admit how I feel about Claudia for a long time, but I've never given her the benefit. I'm a man of few words for most people, even fewer when it comes to my feelings. I don't admit much, not because it wasn't done in our household, but I'm shy. Admitting my feelings means I'm giving over a part of myself to someone else. I've never done that before, and it's scary.

"I wouldn't go that far."

"Why not?"

I shrug, shaking my head. "Because it's the truth. More than anything I was thinking about how you would kick my ass if I didn't stop to help her." No reason to give her any more ammunition than she already has.

She giggles. "You're right. If I knew about it, I would've kicked your ass."

"Exactly, so why are you bustin' my balls about it?"

She folds her hands over her chest, a wistful look on her face, fluttering her lashes in my direction. "Because you're easy to get all worked up."

"And you know this about me because you're my big sister. You're supposed to be nice to me, not trying to piss me off."

She laughs. "The only reason you'd be getting pissed off is because I'm getting too close to the truth. I know you'll never admit it, but it's okay. I don't need you to, I know where you stand."

Shoveling the last of my sandwich in my mouth, I chew and swallow. "If you have nothing else nice to say, I'd appreciate it if you would leave. I have to be up in a few hours."

"You know Dad'll let you open late. There probably won't be many people coming to get their bikes or cars fixed anyway. There's a little over a foot of snow out there."

Fuck. My. Life.

"That's not why I'm worried. If I'm late, I'm sure Dad won't care. I promised to pick up Claudia since I still have her car." I hate admitting that to her. It gives her the ammunition she needs to do a little gossiping with our mom.

"You still have her car? Why are you in her car?" She leans

forward, taking a drink of the water I poured for myself. She's done this since I was a kid, and it's annoyed me from the beginning. It's kind of her way of showing love, but it's still annoying.

"Stop drinking my stuff and, yes, I do still have her car. I have it because, obviously, I had to get back to the house somehow. I don't trust her to be able to drive herself back home, especially with Jay in the car. I offered to come pick them up when she gets off work."

"Look at you," she pauses and licks her lips, twirling around, "being an adult and all that. I'm proud of you, little bro."

"Yeah, yeah, yeah. Could you please leave so I can get a few hours of sleep?" I ask again, trying to keep the exasperation out of my voice.

She snorts. "I'll leave, but I still have many questions, Declan, ones I expect you to answer as soon as you have time." She grabs her jacket and heads toward my front door.

"Sure thing, Riles."

I manage to close the door on her while she's still talking.

Checking the lock, I head to bed, ready for whatever sleep I'm about to get.

CHAPTER 4

CLAUDIA

THIS SHIFT HAS BEEN an absolute shit show. The storm is making it seem as if there's a full moon. They're always the worst. People coming in for the smallest of issues and complaining because they have to wait their turn. Meanwhile, we're expected to keep a smile on our faces and be professional at all times.

Inhaling deeply, I paste one of those smiles on my face as the patient on the stretcher in front of me shakes. He's a frequent flier who's in here because he cut the tip of his finger off. I'm ninety-five percent sure he did it himself so he could get a prescription for painkillers.

"I don't wanna answer any more of your stupid, fuckin' questions," he snarls. "I want this pain to go away. Get me some pain meds, now!"

"I'm not a nurse or a doctor," I remind him through gritted teeth.

"Then get the fuck out."

"Patient gave verbal consent," I mumble under my breath before turning on my heel and walking out of the room.

"People are on one tonight," my co-worker, Jocelyn, groans as we meet up at the nurse's station.

"Girl, at least you're not trying to place IVs while they're fighting and arguing with you," one of the nurses chimes in as she shakes her head.

"I couldn't do it," I declare adamantly. "This is why I'm going to school for accounting. It's something boring and steady."

Jocelyn bumps my shoulder. "That man who drove you to work tonight didn't look boring and steady."

My cheeks heat. "He's my best friend's little brother and was just being nice."

"I wish someone would be that nice to me. My husband didn't even get his lazy ass out of bed to drive me in this weather." The nurse's irritation is palpable.

"Normally, I would've been driving myself. I'm single." I feel the need to explain since I've never had anyone be jealous of me.

"Girl, take it if you can."

Jocelyn looks at me, her eyebrow rising. "Wanna take a lunch break? They've got the cafeteria open since so many of us are here tonight."

My stomach growls, reminding me I haven't eaten in over thirteen hours. "That would be perfect. Can we sneak away?"

She glances up at the board. "Looks like everyone who's come in has been registered. We can't do anything else until they move some patients. Maggie," she says as she looks at the nurse. "Can you let anyone know who's looking for us that we went to take lunch?"

"Sure. Have a good one."

It's nice to turn my badge around, signifying I'm on a break. No questions to answer, no patients to register. The hallways are normally quiet and empty at this time of the morning. It's why I enjoy this shift, although it's harder on my body since it doesn't allow me to get much sleep. What it *does* allow me to do is attend college, where I'll hopefully be able to make a better life for me and Jay.

"Wonder what they have today," I murmur as we enter the cafeteria. It's bustling, just like the hallways. Thankfully, there's an empty table over in the corner. "I'll grab us that seat if you want to go grab your food."

"You sure? I know you and you probably haven't eaten in hours."

"While you're right, I need to text the daycare and make sure Jay's okay."

"Claud, you're allowed to have a life outside of Jay. He's fine here, ya know?" She says the words gently.

"I know."

"Do you?"

"I'm gonna go get our table."

I turn on my heel, effectively cutting her off. Once I get there, I pull my phone out of my pocket. The first conversation is the one I have the most, between myself and the daycare provider for the hospital.

Me: Hey Kristy, I'm just checking on Jay.

Kristy: He's doing good. Asleep.

She sends a picture of him curled up in his toddler bed, tightly holding the bear he loves. I hate that I'll have to leave him with my mom while I attend school. He spends so much time with others watching him. I have to keep reminding myself this is all for the greater good. It won't be like this forever, and one day, I'll be able to be the mother I've always wanted to be.

"Hey, they don't have much," Jocelyn announces as she scoots in across from me. "But this soup looks amazing."

"I'll go grab whatever they have left. I'd eat my arm at this point."

Before she can answer, I'm up and grabbing a tray. As I stand in line, I check my bank account on my phone and see it's dangerously low. Less than twenty bucks, and I don't get paid for two more days. My stomach drops, but I switch over to my account from the hospital. I put money on it with every paycheck and use it sparingly. Finally, something is going right tonight. I have thirty bucks on the account, and with my discount, I'll be able to have a good dinner, including dessert.

Without the guilt I normally feel, I get a full meal and then head on over to have a seat with Jocelyn.

"Look at you, finally eating enough to put some meat on your bones," she teases, a smile on her face.

"I know, I know. It was time, right?"

"You know if you need some help, I'm here. If there's one thing I can do, it's buy your lunch every once in a while. I was a single mom when my kids were little. If anyone knows how hard it is, it's me."

The soup is hot and warms my body as it goes down. I've been cold since I was stuck outside, trying to move my car. This is a welcome reprieve.

"So... that guy who drove you into work?"

I roll my eyes. "You've been trying to get me to date since I started working here."

"You're a beautiful girl who works too hard and needs to let her hair down," she argues.

"I'm the single mother of a three-year-old who hasn't had her hair cut or dyed in two years, and I still haven't lost the final twenty pounds I gained when I was pregnant. There are permanent dark circles under my eyes, and I can't tell you the last time I wore makeup. Joce, I'm not in any shape to catch the eye of either gender."

She laughs. "You really don't know, do you?"

"Know what?"

She puts her spoon down and motions for me to do the same. "You're one of the most beautiful women I've ever seen. There's this wounded gorgeousness to you. Speaking from experience, anyone who looks at you just wants to make things better. A guy who looks like that? He was doing more than just a favor for his sister."

While I'd love to believe what she's saying, I can't.

If I do, then I'll start to think I deserve things I should never have asked for.

CHAPTER 5
DECLAN

I'M outside when Claudia walks out, carrying Jay in her arms. He looks well-rested while she appears to be exhausted. Getting out, I open the back door for her and then wait while she gets him settled.

"Dec!" he screeches, reaching out his arms to me. I've not been around him a ton, but he does know who I am because of Riley and Claudia hanging out all the time.

"Hey," I reply, ruffling his hair. "Did you have a good sleep?" It's the same thing I ask my cat when he wakes up in the morning and stretches while sticking his ass in my face. Seems like the appropriate thing to do.

"Yeah, but I woke up hungry."

His voice is so small.

"Jay, we'll grab something when we get home," Claudia cuts in.

"If you're not too tired, I'd like to stop." I glance over at her. "I'm pretty hungry myself. My treat." I shrug, making it look as innocent as I can. I don't want her to think I'm offering her charity. I know how she feels about it. Every time my mom tries to give her something, she almost always declines.

"You've already done so much," she argues.

I reach in, putting Jay in his car seat. "You wanna check to make sure I did it right?" I ask, moving back out of the way. "And I haven't done anything I wouldn't do for someone else who's a friend that needs help. I know you think I'm doing this because of Riley and your relationship with her, but like I told you earlier, I don't do shit I don't want to. I don't feel sorry for you. I think you're a damn strong woman who's scared to let others help you."

When she stands up, she has a smile on her face. "You put him in the car seat correctly. His dad can't even do that, and I'm trying to be easier with myself, accepting help when others offer it."

"You could stand to do that better," I tease and give her a grin.

She reaches out, playfully punching me in the stomach. "Oh, I get it. You're gonna call me on my shit, huh?"

"Someone needs to. C'mon, I'm starving. I tried to eat a snack last night, but Riley was at my place when I got home and she was annoying as fuck."

"Always the big sister, huh?" Claudia grins affectionately.

"She realized I wasn't home and it was late, or early, depending on how you want to take it. She wanted to make sure I was okay."

"You're lucky to have her," she says wistfully. "We both are."

"Let's go."

I move ahead slightly and open the door, motioning for her to get in. As I walk around the car, I think about how damn tired she looks. I take a seat behind the wheel. "Do you have class today?"

"This afternoon," she sighs. "I'm hoping to get a few hours' sleep before I have to be there."

"Who watches Jay while you do that?" I back up and put the car in gear, driving toward my favorite breakfast spot.

"My mom. She's retired due to an on-the-job injury, but she's still able to take care of Jay when I need her to, and he loves his Mimi. I try not to overburden her, but she's one of the only people I trust with my son."

We're quiet for a few minutes as I concentrate on getting the car out of this fucking parking lot. It's barely been cleared and salted. A hospital should do a better job since people are coming here with emergent issues. If I worked here or had any pull, I would give them a piece of my mind.

"What about you?" she asks.

"What about me, what?"

"When do you have to be at work? Are you giving up a bunch of your time in order to help us?" she questions.

"I don't want you to make a special trip or have to work late because you've decided to get some good karma," she teases.

"Whenever I'm done. Like I told you last night, I've started taking over a lot of the work, which means I can make my own hours or work later into the night if I want to."

"It makes me feel bad to know you're going to have to work later because you're doing something for me."

I groan in the back of my throat. "Every time you say something like that, I'm going to kiss your cheek to let you know you don't have to fucking apologize for life."

She chuckles. "Maybe I do need something like that to help me stop apologizing."

"You don't have to be sorry for the life you've created, Claudia. It would be hard for anyone, and you don't have to pretend it should be easier than it is."

I wonder if I've overstepped my boundaries when she

doesn't talk anymore. As we drive down the road, Jay is making noises in his car seat, and as he sees the sign for one of my favorite breakfast spots, yells, "Pancakes!" and claps his hands.

"Is that what you want for breakfast?" I question, looking at him through the rearview mirror.

"Pancakes and bacon," he answers.

"Then that's what you're going to have."

Jockeying the car into the morning rush hour, I find us a spot in traffic and then immediately turn into the parking lot. We all get out and Jay reaches for me. It warms my heart in a way I can't begin to explain. I lift him up in my arms, settling him on my hip before adjusting the beanie on his head. Claudia reaches into the back and grabs his diaper bag. Before I know it, we're inside and seated.

"Have you ever had a meal with a toddler?" Claudia asks, looking at me with wide eyes. "And I don't mean at your house. I mean out in a restaurant."

"No," I admit. "I'm the youngest and they stopped after me. You know as well as I do that Riley doesn't have kids – or even think about having them."

"Then you're in for a treat," she giggles.

I have no idea what she means until the food comes, and although Jay had been talking about being hungry, he plays with it instead of eating it and whining when Claudia admonishes him and tries to feed him. She sighs, putting her fork down and motioning for him to get over into her lap. How many times has she had to do this on her own? "I'll take him." I reach over, grabbing him before he can get in her lap. He begins to play with his food again, but I make a noise in the back of my throat. "No, we don't play with our food. You eat it or you don't get it at all."

Surprisingly he listens, and begins eating without playing.

"I've never seen him listen to someone so quickly," she comments, taking a drink of her orange juice.

"It's because I'm not his parent. Kids tend to listen to others better."

"Isn't that the damn truth?"

And with those words, we go about eating our breakfast quietly.

CHAPTER 6
CLAUDIA

IT'S BEEN three days since Declan saved us, and I haven't seen him since. I find myself looking for him throughout the day, even if we were only together for a few hours. It was nice to have someone to back me up when Jay was having a hard time listening to me.

"What's that look on your face?" Jocelyn asks as we sit in the break room.

It's been a pretty easy night, which I'm scared to admit, but it is what it is. I have my laptop out, catching up on some of the reading and weekly assignments I've been putting off. This doesn't happen very often, but when it does, I'm very grateful. It's uninterrupted time that I don't usually get, so I take it as a gift. "Nothing, just thinking."

"If I were you, I'd still be thinking about that man who dropped you off earlier this week."

I slam my hand down on my notebook. "It's like you're in my brain. How do you always do this?"

"Because I'm the person you don't allow yourself to be," she giggles.

"I don't think I've ever heard a more accurate description of our relationship. Anyway, he gave me his number to text him when he drove us in, but is it appropriate to text him just because I wanna know what he's doing?"

"I think it's appropriate whenever you wanna text him. I'd be texting him all the time... asking him for pictures of those tattoos." She's got her brow quirked and a smirk across her face.

"That's not why I want to text him," I deny and roll my eyes.

"Then why do you? Inquiring minds wanna know."

"To thank him and see how he's doing."

"Isn't his sister your best friend? You could send that message through her. Don't give me that line of horse shit. You might believe it, but I don't believe it for one second."

And she shouldn't. There are a bunch of things I'd like to talk to him about. "Whatever, I've got work to do."

"I've got a snack to go get," she groans. "I don't keep these hips by dieting."

When she leaves, I pick up my phone and think about texting Declan, but instead, I text Riley.

> Me: How's your day?

> R: Fucking long. I'm working at the shop after getting off from my day job. I can't wait until we can hire somebody to run these books and do this inventory. When do you graduate again?

> Me: LOL! You know this is my last semester, but what makes you think I'll accept?

> R: Free daycare, an amazing boss, great pay, and crazy good benefits.

Me: Okay, you've got me. If the shop still needs someone in four months, I'll be there. I don't work at the hospital tomorrow. Do you want me to come and help with the inventory?

R: That would be great. It's just me and Dec. Everyone else has other things to do.

Me: I'll be there. Five?

R: Yeah. Do you need to bring Jay with you? Mom would love to watch him.

Me: If she doesn't mind. I'd like to give mine a break.

R: See you tomorrow!

Me: See ya.

And just like that, I can see how Declan is without having to text him. Maybe life does work in mysterious ways.

"LET me just close the bay and turn the light out," Trick is saying as I enter the shop. "Then I'll leave it to the rest of you."

"Hey." Riley waves over at me. "How's Jay man?" She runs toward us, holding her arms out.

"Riley!" he squeals and jumps up into her arms.

I love their relationship. I'm an only child, and if I had the chance to have a sister, it would definitely be Riley. She treats him like her own nephew, buys him gifts, watches him when I need help, and when his dad left me in the delivery room on my own, she was there when I gave birth.

"You ready to spend time with Had Had? She's got spaghetti for you, and I heard she made cupcakes for dessert."

That's the name he gave to Riley and Declan's mom the first time he'd been able to say it. I'm not sure he's ever said Hadley. "Be sure and tell her thank you," I instruct him as they head up the stairs.

Declan comes out of the office, looking like a damn model for some blue-collar calendar. It's obvious he's had a long day. Grease covers his arms and portions of his face. The shirt he wears was once white, but is now gray and almost black in certain places. His hands are clean, though, which I've always noticed about him. No matter how dirty his hands get during the day, by the time it's the end, he's made sure his nails and hands are clean. "Claud, I thought I heard you. Thanks for offering to help us."

"It's what friends are for, right?"

"Just so long as it's not as a thank you for helping you the other day. I won't accept it," he smirks, crossing his arms over his chest.

Normally, I don't let my thoughts take on a female gaze because I just don't have the time to take a long bath with a vibrator, much less build a relationship and get close enough to a man to fulfill any needs I might have. But, fuck me; the way his biceps bulge is enough to make me rethink the long bath with a vibrator. "It's not." I roll my lips together. "I'm doing this as a favor to Riley, not you."

"Fuckin' ouch." He grabs for his heart. "That hurt. Damn girl, you're more sassy than I thought."

I laugh, biting my bottom lip. "I've just never felt comfortable enough to tease you, but now that you've helped me, you've crossed over."

"I'm flattered."

"As you should be."

"Touché."

Riley comes back down just then. "Mom's got Jay eating the

biggest plate of spaghetti I've ever seen a toddler eat, and Dad is talking to him in that stupid baby voice he gets. It almost makes my womb ache."

"They're really good with him, and I'm so thankful for it."

"He was the same with me when I was little," Riley admits with a grin.

"How do you even remember that?" Declan asks, wrinkling his brow.

Have they never told him that he and Riley are half-brother and sister? I decide it's not my place when Riley answers.

"I've always had a better memory than you. Who helps you remember Mother's Day and Father's Day every year?" she argues.

"We're wasting valuable time," I remind them. "Let's get this going so we can count these screws."

Declan walks with a slow swagger over to the fridge. "Anyone want a beer? Gonna be a long night. You can eat before you leave," he says, tipping the bottle toward me.

Fuck it. "Hand it over."

Riley takes one too, and when Declan cranks up a radio, we all get to work doing the inventory.

CHAPTER 7
DECLAN

SIX HOURS later and we're all upstairs eating the leftover spaghetti cold. It's one of the best meals I've ever had. It may be because I'm starving, or maybe it's because of who I'm sitting with. We had a few more beers, and I'm not sure I should send Jay and Claudia home tonight. Her eyes are glassy and her smile is as bright as the damn sun. I wish this is how she could be all the time. At the moment, she looks like a young girl having a good time with a few friends.

"You dropped that on your shirt," she giggles, pointing at my chest.

"Not like it's going to make a difference. I mean, I don't even know what color it's supposed to be. It's been years since I actually knew what color shirts I'm wearing when I'm in the shop."

"Maybe you should eat some more food," Riley encourages and points to Claudia's plate. "It's been a while since you've had a few drinks, and I think it's affecting you more than you think it is."

She stops smiling and immediately starts eating more food.

"Damn, Riles, let her have some fun. You can stay with me.

I have an extra bedroom," I offer, as I take another pull from my beer.

"She can always stay with me, but she'll have to sleep with me," Riley argues.

"Seeing as how you kick like a damn kangaroo, she might like my empty bed a little better."

"You two can stop talking about me like I'm not here. What would I do with Jay?" Mom's voice comes from over our shoulders. "He can stay right where he is. I know that sometimes a mom just needs a night off. He'll be well taken care of, no matter which of my kids you decide to stay with. You can even stay with us, but you'll either have to take the couch or the bed your son is sleeping in."

"Thank you so much, Hadley. If there's anything I can ever do for you, please let me know."

"I'm not offering because I expect something in return, I hope you know that. All I want to do is help out someone I see as a third child."

She nods, rubbing her lips together. "I'll stay with him." She tilts her head at me. "He's right, Riles. Last time I slept with you, I ended up with bruises on my legs that looked like I'd been beaten."

Riley snorts. "Never had a man complain before."

"That's because they were getting something they wanted," Claudia quips.

"There she is again." I tilt my beer bottle over toward her. "I've been finding out this one can be a little hellcat when she wants to be."

"It's true. She just doesn't show it often."

As she's about to respond to us, a loud yawn escapes her mouth. "Would you like to go to sleep?"

"If you don't mind. All the beers I've drunk have made me

so sleepy. I'm not tipsy, I promise, just relaxed. It's not like you're going to have to take care of me."

I grab our plates. "We'll finish this later. Come on, Sleeping Beauty."

As we head down the steps into the shop so that I can get to my side of the building, she speaks.

"It's really cool how this is like some sort of complex your whole family has built. It must be cool to be this close to them all the time."

"I mean, it is until it isn't. Remember me telling you that Riley showed up at like three in the morning to check on me? Over the past few years, Mom and Dad have learned to give me space, but it's hard for her."

"Because she's taken care of you since y'all were little."

"Yeah, she thinks she's my second mother." I grin over my shoulder. We climb another set of stairs and then we're at the front door to my apartment. I punch in the number on my keypad and step aside so she can come in. "You're in luck. I just changed the sheets in the guest room the other day. I had a buddy stay over for the Super Bowl, and he got messy drunk."

"Please don't go to any trouble," she says, shaking her head.

"Do you want another one?" I point to the beer in my hand. "I won't tell or think any less of you if you do."

"Not a beer. Do you have any bourbon?" A slow smile spreads across my face.

"You like bourbon?"

"I only drink it on occasion, but yeah, I do."

"Me, too. I'm always on the search for the best I can find. The more expensive, the better. If I could find a Pappy Van Winkle for less than five grand around here, I would give my left nut."

She giggles loudly. "So you have a collection? Does that mean I get to pick which one I want?"

"You definitely can. Let me show you." I walk her over to my cabinet. When I open it, she makes a sound in the back of her throat.

"Oh, this is a good collection. How long have you been at it?"

"Dad gave me my first one when I turned eighteen. He noticed I had an affinity for bourbon, although I really shouldn't have been drinking anything. Now everyone gets it for me on special occasions. So please tell me which one you want, my Lady."

Her cheeks turn a bright shade of pink and she pulls her bottom lip between her teeth. "Elijah Craig, Small Batch."

Raising an eyebrow, I pick it up and present it to her. "Great choice. You have good taste."

"I know." She tilts her head, giving me a smile.

Walking us over to the island I use as a kitchen table, I grab two glasses and put them down in front of us. "You want some water with it?"

"Yeah, I like a little bit less than a fifty/fifty ratio, but since it's a smooth one, I'll take thirty percent water."

"Listen to you, wanting percentages."

She giggles, taking a sip. "What about you?"

"I take mine straight."

"Tell me something about yourself, Declan. One thing that no one knows about you."

I twirl my drink around in the glass. "I tell you something, you tell me something?"

She takes a drink and nods. "Promise."

"One of my biggest goals in life is to be a dad, whether it be biologically or not. I see what kind of a father I have and I've seen the type of father other people have. I'd love to be able to teach a child of mine everything my dad taught me."

She swallows roughly. "You're a good man, Declan, and you're going to make someone very happy one day."

I take another drink, liquid courage perhaps. "I hope you don't think bad of me if I tell you I've kinda hoped that is you since I realized what it was for a guy to recognize a girl in a certain way."

She inhales deeply. "Then it won't be weird for me to tell you the only thing I've thought about since I got here was how hot you look in that dirty t-shirt.'"

CHAPTER 8

CLAUDIA

I CAN'T BELIEVE those words just came out of my mouth. That isn't me, not normally. Could it be the alcohol or the loneliness talking? "I'm sorry," I mutter, ducking my head. "I shouldn't have said that. It probably feels slightly disgusting coming from your older sister's best friend. I'm eight years older than you are."

"No," he moves forward, putting his index finger under my chin. "I've never thought of you that way. If anything, I've always thought of you as unattainable; someone who was much better than me, and way more put together than I ever will be."

I giggle, surprised at how he sees me, because I see myself so much differently than he does. "Having it together? I am barely keeping my head above water most days. It's a struggle... All of it. When I look at you, I see someone who's got everything going for them. You'll have the family business, and you'll continue to grow it in ways others probably never thought about."

He doesn't remove his finger from my chin. and I let myself lean further into him, enjoying the touch. It's been so long since

I felt a touch other than my own. His throat clears roughly. "But that's not all I want," he shrugs. "I look at you, and I want to be a part of your family with Jay. I'm the type of guy who's always wanted to be settled. I don't fuck around with women a lot. It's been months since I've even been on a date."

"Months? Try over a year," I laugh.

"What was your last date?" he asks, moving his finger from under my chin, opening his palm against the back of my neck. "You can tell me anything."

Swallowing roughly, I debate on whether or not to tell him the truth of what I did a little over a year ago. "Like you, I was lonely and I just wanted a touch from someone who wasn't myself. One night I was so fucking horny, and I just needed it."

"There's nothing wrong with that," he interrupts. "We all have needs. Doesn't matter if you're a single mother with a child, or just some college girl who wants to have a good time. Hell, I have needs, and I troll the bars."

Tilting my head into his touch, I let all my secrets spill. "I went on Tinder, and I let the person know it was about one thing, and one thing only. I made up a lie and had my mom watch Jay, used the last of what I had on a credit card to rent a room at a mid-level hotel and invited him over. We fucked three times that night, but I felt so dirty afterwards. I couldn't sleep there when he left. I ended up going home and taking a shower for over an hour. I was exhausted, so I slept the rest of the night, and when I woke up to go get Jay, I told myself I'd never do it again."

"First of all, you can do anything you want to do. You're an adult who knows what she needs. There's no reason you should feel bad about it. It doesn't make you a bad person, mom, or anything like that. You're human, and that's okay."

"Where do I go from here, though?" I ask, "Because I still have needs, and I'm still denying myself because I don't know how to be a mom and a woman. I've been a single mother since I had Jay. I don't know how to live my life and be a mom without having guilt."

He adjusts his stance, spreading his legs apart so that he can look into my eyes. He brings both palms up to my cheeks, holding my face. "What I'm about to say to you I want you to hear, and I desperately want you to feel."

I nod, there's nothing else I can do. When he speaks, I tend to listen. "Okay."

"I want you to understand what I'm saying is coming straight from my heart. I don't want you to take it any way other than that. Don't let it get into your head, and just tell me the first answer that comes into your head."

"You're starting to make me nervous," I admit, my mouth dry.

"See – stop that. I'm gonna be incredibly honest with you, since you were with me. When I was a teenager, you were the first girl I ever jacked off thinking about. To this day, if I even date a girl, they're going up against what I know of you. So what I'm saying to you is this, Claud. You need to get off? You want someone to scratch your itch? If that bed is cold and lonely, then you can come to me, and I'll take care of you."

I'm not only speechless, but incredibly hot as fuck, especially with the low octave his voice has dropped to.

My throat is as dry as the Sahara. "You... you... don't have to offer," I stutter.

"It's not a hardship for me, if that's what you're thinking. I just told you the thoughts I've had about you. If anyone should be embarrassed here, it's me."

Inhaling deeply, I pull my bottom lip in between my teeth, trying to ignore how wet I am between my thighs, and how much that patch of skin aches for not just any touch, but his.

"I'm not embarrassed," I admit, tugging at the collar of my sweatshirt. "I'm fucking hot."

He steps closer, his mouth tilting over mine. "Then let me help you take care of that heat."

"What happens when we're around your family? What does this mean? Are we friends with benefits? Is this a relationship?" Internally I'm freaking out, but the way I ache between my thighs shows I'm giving thought to this.

"Whatever you want. We can be friends with benefits, and you will definitely drive the way this goes."

I've had so little that's mine in the past few years, I desperately want something that makes me not just a mother, or a student burning the candle at both ends, I want to be a woman. The type of woman I was before I became responsible for another life. I want this more than I should, and it's being dangled in front of me. Closing my eyes, I speak words I know will change not only mine and Declan's relationship, but mine and Riley's too. "I want it," I whisper. "I want you. I want to feel like a woman instead of just a mother and student. Please, make me feel something other than this loneliness and ache. Make it go away," I beg.

"If you're sure," he whispers back to me.

"I am."

"Whenever you want this to stop, you let me know. I promise I won't do anything you don't want. You're safe with me."

"I know, which is exactly why I'm willing to give this a shot." I reach down, crossing my arms at the hem of my sweatshirt, and pull it over my head. "Make me feel good, Declan. I'm begging you."

CHAPTER 9

DECLAN

MY BODY HARDENS as hers is exposed to me. A siren is hidden underneath the bulky clothing she normally wears. Full tits are barely held back by lace edges. The milky white skin begs for my touch, and I can't stop myself from reaching out and taking what I want. Goosebumps pop up as I trail my fingertip across the supple skin. "What do you want me to do, Claud?" I ask, voice tight with need. The silence in the room still somehow manages to cover up the intense thumping of my heart. At the same time, I can see her pulse against her neck. We're both nervous, but I refuse to let those nerves get the better of either of us.

She licks her lips, punching her head back. "Make me feel good, Declan. Don't make me put it into words. I don't know if I can do that."

Leaning down, I tilt my head, catching my nose on hers. "You don't have to beg me; just wanna make sure you're okay with this."

"Beyond okay," she answers on a gust of air.

"That's all I needed to hear."

My eyes flutter before I take one more look at her and capture her lips with mine. I'll remember this moment forever. I've thought about what it would be like to kiss her since I knew what that feeling in the pit of my stomach was when she would come around. The kiss I initiate is slow and thorough. I work my way around her mouth, making sure I touch every piece of real estate. She moans, twisting her fingers in my shirt, holding tightly as she sways in my arms.

"It's not the alcohol," she promises, "it's the lack of air. Anybody ever told you you're a great kisser?"

"Not really, but I'm trying to impress you. I hope it's working." I put my hands at her hips before rolling them back over her ass, lifting her in the air, and guiding her legs around my waist. The spot in between her thighs is warm, even touching this way.

She tightens her thighs, holding on tightly as I walk us back to my bedroom, and place her gently on the bed. When she looks up at me, her eyes are so fucking trusting. "If they've not told you what a great kisser you are, then surely they've told you how hot you are?"

"You're hotter than I am," I chuckle, wondering if she'll ever see herself the way I see her.

"Negative," she laughs along with me.

Her hands sneak over to me, grasping the hem of my t-shirt, and slowly peeling it up and over my head. Carefully, she runs her nails down my chest and abdomen until she gets to the top of my jeans. Her hazel eyes sneak up to mine, holding mischief and seduction in equal parts. This is who I've always imagined her being. She smirks as she reaches for the button on my Levi's. I let her play for a few more minutes before I press her back into the sheets, covering her body with mine.

Leveraging myself over her, I press up on my hands before settling back on my knees. Leaning down, I pull one of the cups of her bra down, exposing her nipple to my gaze. It tightens further the longer I look. My mouth waters before I bend down and take the peak into my mouth, running my tongue against the tip. Her fingers tangle in my hair, holding me to her.

"Yes, Dec, don't stop," she whimpers as I move over to the other one.

"I'll keep going as long as you need me to."

She presses her lips together, before pulling them apart, licking the dryness away. "If that's the case, then I'm never going to want you to stop. But I do want you to know, I don't think I can handle sex tonight."

"Regardless of how hard my cock is, it didn't cross my mind. All I want is to make you feel like a woman."

"Then please, proceed," she giggles.

"With pleasure." I nuzzle at her neck, before making a straight line down her body. Encountering the waistband of her leggings, I slip my fingers under the elastic, before lifting my gaze up to hers.

Hers is heated as our eyes meet. She swallows roughly. "It's been a really long time," she whispers. "I haven't shaved in over a year."

"Are you uncomfortable?" I question, noticing the way she's frozen.

"With you doing that? Yeah."

As quickly as I went down, I come back up. "Then I won't do it."

She nods, wrapping her arms around my neck, burying her face in the curve. "Sorry."

"No, no, there is no reason for you to be sorry. This is about you, and if that's not comfortable for you, then we won't be doing that," I assure her. "But I think you would be more comfortable if we could get your leggings off, huh?"

She rolls her lips. "I can't believe you know what they are."

"I have a sister who involves me in every aspect of her life."

Throwing her head back, she giggles. I take that moment to move her leggings off her body. It's safe to say I'm not pushing her. Instead of putting my fingers behind the cotton of her panties, I run the back of my knuckle along the covered seam of her pussy.

"Fuck, Declan. How can that feel so good?"

"Let yourself enjoy it, Claudia.

Her exhale is shaky. That's when I notice her hands leaving my body. She reaches out, grabbing hold of the covers, her arms tightening as she hangs on. Her legs fall further apart, and I know she's finally relaxed. Sneaking my fingers passed the edge of her panties, I slowly rub the blunt tip of my middle finger down her slit. She's soaking wet, and almost immediately she thrusts toward me. Bending down, I grasp her nipple with my lips, sucking as I hook my index and middle fingers into her body, using my thumb at her clit.

She grinds against me, her breath hitching. "Declan, God, I want this so much."

Removing my mouth from her nipple, I glance up, loving the look on her face. "Take it, sweet girl. Take what the fuck you need."

She does, moving harder and faster into my touch.

Her body tightens.

Tightens.

Tightens.

Until she screams, becoming liquid in my arms.

And at the same time, becoming the most beautiful woman I've ever seen.

CHAPTER 10

CLAUDIA

THE AFTERMATH of being pleasured by Declan is more than I ever could have imagined. His arms are wrapped tightly around me, and my heart is pounding in my chest. His cock presses heavily into my ass, but I don't feel an obligation or want to reciprocate. A loud yawn cracks my jaw.

"Go to sleep, Claud. Jay is safe with my parents, and you're safe with me. For once you don't have to worry that everything's going to be done. You don't have to be a light sleeper just in case your son gets up in the middle of the night and needs something. We've got you, Claud. You're a part of this family and you're not going to be able to get rid of that anytime soon. I mean who would want to? We love your kid as much as you do. Now that you're in the Tennyson fold, good luck getting out."

It sounds better than I ever imagined it would. It sounds like one of the best things anyone has ever done for me, and I'm all in. No matter how quickly it's happening, I, of all people, know how quick life can change, and adapting is a gift I'm learning all too well I have.

I can't remember the last time I went to sleep without the dread of the next day sitting heavily in my stomach. But tonight? I close my eyes and the next thing I know, I'm waking back up.

Given the position I'm in, I don't think I moved at all last night. Declan's strong arms are still wrapped tightly around my waist. In a replay of what happened a few hours ago, his morning wood is pressed against my back. But this time, I'm much more comfortable in my role. His breath moves the hair at my neck at a steady rhythm. This time it's more arousal than satisfying. The decision is made before I even realize it. My hand is reaching back between us, grasping hold of his length.

My touch is slow at first, getting acquainted with his body. The organ is strong, lengthening even more as I start a slow stroke up and down. He moans into my neck, his arms stretching out to grasp the pillow. His arms are hot as fuck, the muscles bulging and the ink standing out in stark relief as he grips the sheet.

His hips swing, helping me move up and down on his cock, but his underwear is annoying. At some point last night he got rid of his jeans, and now I want to feel the flesh behind the cotton fabric of his boxer briefs. "Take 'em off," I whisper hotly.

There's no hesitation.

He does what I ask, groaning deeply in his throat as my bare hand wraps around his equally bare cock. His breath is hot against my neck, his forehead beading with sweat. Before I know what's happening, he's let go of the sheet with one hand and hitched my thigh up over his leg, exposing me to his touch.

A finger slips inside my swollen flesh as I work him. We're thrusting against each other in different rhythms. My leg is shaking, the bed is squeaking, and his broken breaths are fucking *everything* to me.

I've never wanted an orgasm as bad as I want this one, not

even the one last night. Last night felt like a gimme, where I got back on the horse, so to speak. This one is more like I'm finding myself underneath all the bagginess I've hidden myself under.

The shirts.

My son.

Not feeling deserving of anything because I'm a single mother who should put all of her time and energy into making a better life for her child.

All that shit is gone in this moment. None of that is in the back of my mind. All that matters right now is that I'm a woman who wants to make a man cum, and wants it for herself too.

"Fuck, sweet girl," he moans as he tugs on the edge of my ear with his teeth.

It's the name he called me last night, too. My pussy clenches, No one has ever had a name for me before, not like this, and not muttered in the guttural tone of a man who sounds as if he's hanging on by a thread.

To know I have this man so close to exploding is not only empowering, but one of the biggest turn-ons I've ever experienced. To feel him thrusting against me, knowing it's my body that's bringing him pleasure?

Fuck, yes.

Sign me up.

"I'm so close." The words are like a mantra chanted at my ear. The fresh scrape of his morning beard is like sandpaper against my throat, but that little bit of sting makes my nipples hard and my pussy wetter.

"Me too," I answer, spreading my legs further apart, needing this desperately.

He sucks at the side of my neck as he splashes against my back. That's all I need to reach my own climax.

When it's over, we lay together, each gasping air into our

depleted lungs.

And I know nothing between us will ever be the same again.

CHAPTER 11
DECLAN

EVERYONE CAN TELL.

She's glowing, and I'm almost positive I have love bites on my neck. Maybe I should've checked before I left the apartment. There's also a chance no one knows what happened between us last night, but I don't think that's the case. They're all looking at us.

At least that's the way it seems. Maybe it's because I feel her in my bones. I always knew as soon as she allowed me to taste her, that would be it for me.

And it is.

Fucking game over for me.

"Do you want pancakes?" Mom asks from where she stands in the kitchen, her back to the rest of us.

"Two," I reply, holding up the corresponding fingers.

"Coming right up. Claudia, go over there and sit down. Enjoy your son, and let me make you breakfast."

"Hadley, I don't mind helping," Claudia argues.

"I know you don't, but I was a single mom once, and I know

how hard it is to get time for yourself. Go watch some shitty TV with my kids and husband."

My ears perk up. "What do you mean by single mom?" In my twenty-four years I've never heard this, and I have no idea what they're talking about.

Dad clears his throat, turning the TV down. Our cat, Tux the Third comes over, and takes a seat in my lap. I let him give me the comfort he's offering, and turn my attention back to my dad. "Is there something I need to know?"

He rubs at his chin. "There wasn't ever really a good time to tell you, I guess. We always said we would tell you when you asked, but you never did."

"Asked what?" Now I'm more confused than ever.

"Dad adopted me," Riley answers. "He came into my life when I was young. Six. I still remember the outfit I was wearing on the day I met him; a plain white t-shirt, a black ruffled tutu, and my pink Converse sneakers. It was my favorite outfit, and I knew on the day I was going to meet the man who was going to be my Companion, I had to put my best foot forward," she smiles at our Dad.

"Let me explain," Dad says as he hunches over, putting his elbows on his knees. "I'd gotten in trouble. Done some shit I shouldn't have done, and got hit with a felony."

"You?" My eyes bug out of my head. "A felon?"

"Yeah. Like I said, I did some shit I shouldn't have done. In order to not have to serve anymore jail time, I was given community service, and placed in what was called The Companion Care program. It placed men and women, who weren't dangerous felons, with kids who needed an adult figure in their lives. I was paired with Riley." He looks over at my sister, smiling brightly at her. "Pretty quickly I fell in love with both Riley and your mom. We got married, I adopted Riles, and we had you. Now we're one big, happy family."

"What about her biological dad?" I question, needing to know the rest of the story.

Mom speaks up. "Trick loves her more than he ever did. It was a bad situation with him. He wasn't cut out to be Riley's father, but Trick was from the moment he met her."

Riley grins, her eyes bright. "When he asked mom to marry him, he asked me if he could be my dad. I knew there was no doubt in my mind."

"We never meant to keep that from you," Mom sighs. "Like your dad said, you just never asked."

"And I've not once ever thought of Riles as my adopted daughter and you my biological son. It's not a big deal to me, so I've not made it one to anyone else. I'm sorry if you feel like we kept a big secret from you," he shrugs. "It was never my intention."

"No, I don't feel that way at all. Riley's my sister, always has been. I think it's pretty badass that you adopted her."

Dad grins. "Figured you would," he says, pointedly looking between Claudia and myself.

I tilt my head to the side, giving him a glare. "Thanks for explaining it to me."

"Whatever questions you have, just ask them."

Mom puts a bunch of plates on the table, interrupting the conversation. "But as you ask them, please come get your breakfast."

Claudia grabs Jay up in her arms, bringing him to the table, as the rest of us follow behind. She sits next to Riley as she normally does when she's over, but Jay has a seat in between me and Dad.

Riley grins over at him. "Wanna be with the big dudes, huh?"

He flexes his muscles while the rest of us laugh, and I have to wonder how often he's been given the chance to be the little boy he is.

I vow right now to let him have more of those moments. When I look at him now, I see my big sister as a little girl, and I want to be the person to him that our dad was to her.

CHAPTER 12
CLAUDIA

"YOU'RE good to drive yourself home?" Declan asks as I finish packing the bag I carry with Jay wherever I go.

"I am," I nod, giving him a nervous smile.

My heart is pounding so hard, I'm surprised he can't hear it. Being near him right now, after last night, is like an awakening. A fluttering in my stomach I've never had before causes my hands to shake. He walks up behind me, and the woodsy smell of his cologne invades my senses. "Do you want me to follow you? Make sure things are okay?"

"No," I reply and shake my head. "We've got it. I really appreciate what you've done for us."

"Why do I feel like I'm getting the brush off here?" He moves so that he's standing in front of me, and I'm not able to avoid his gaze.

"It's not a brush off," I assure him. "It's the fact I'm the mother of a young child, I'm older than you are, and I have responsibilities you don't have. The past two days have been fun, but they're a bubble, Declan. It's not reality."

He jerks back as if he's been slapped. "It could easily be our reality."

I look over to Jay and see he's coloring, not paying attention to us at all. It gives me the courage to say what's on my mind. I smile sadly. "No it couldn't. This is fun for you. It's not your life, but it is mine. I don't get involved with men. I refuse to let them come in and out of his life, the way men have come in and out of mine. You're young – I mean you were coming home from the bar when you found us. It's a lot to ask of you to take us on."

"Nobody's asking me to do anything, Claud, least of all you, and I'm honestly fucking offended you think I wouldn't take it seriously."

My stomach clenches as I notice the pink spots on his cheeks. "I don't mean to make you angry."

"I'm not angry," he argues. "You've known me since I was born..."

"Which is another problem," I add. I'm starting to spiral, I can feel it coming. "The age difference between us."

"It makes no difference to me, either way," he interrupts. "If you were younger than me, I wouldn't disregard what you want, or your feelings."

"Look," I blow a breath toward my long bangs. "The most important thing in my life is Jay. I have to think of him before anything else."

He steps closer, hooking his fingers in the edges of my sweatshirt and pulls me into him. "I think we proved last night you do have needs. They shouldn't be ignored. In order for you to be a good mother for your son, you can't live like a nun, Claud."

"You don't understand."

Unexpected tears spring to my eyes, ones I've held back for

far too long. Usually I'm able to push them to the side, but these leak out, running silently down my face.

Those tattooed arms of his cross over his chest. "I think I do understand. Because you feel as if you don't deserve anything, you're willing to punish yourself."

Inhaling deeply, I grab up Jay's bag. "It's not about punishing myself, and I don't expect you to understand. But he's my responsibility," I point at Jay. "His dad? He does nothing, not even what he should. Not even the fucking bare minimum. He deserves someone who will go above and beyond, Dec. If his dad won't do it, then I will."

"What if I want to? You're making decisions for me without giving me the benefit of the doubt. I'm a responsible person, Claudia. I'm helping my dad run this business. In two years it's going to be mine. Of course G will help, but I'll be responsible for making enough money for the family. It's a lot to explain, but the fact you don't trust me? It hurts."

"Why should that hurt you? You haven't proven it to me," I hiss.

"On the same token, you haven't asked," he hisses back at me. "You want me to prove it to you? I'll do that."

This takes me aback. No one has ever offered to prove it before. "I'll give you a couple of weeks. If something seems off, then I'm out. I have to protect not only myself, but Jay too."

He shoves his fingers through his hair. "Okay, maybe I came on too strong, wanna prove myself too much. I've liked you longer than I care to admit," he ducks his head, "whether you've known it or not. I've watched you, saw you struggle with his dad, and heard you cry to Riley. I wanted to go punch him in his motherfuckin' jaw because of what he did to you."

No one has ever stood up for me like this. Not even my mom. When I told her I was pregnant, she accused me of being stupid.

Having seen how hard it was for her when my dad left, I should've known better. As if I hadn't said all this same shit to myself. All I needed was her support, but instead, I was ridiculed. The only reason I believe she helps me now is because she loves Jay, which is why I never take it for granted. I want to believe Declan, want to give him a chance, but I'm scared. More scared than I've ever been.

But don't they always say fear pushes us to make choices we might not make otherwise? "Okay," I sigh. "I'll give you a chance."

He leans in, kissing my lips softly, so different from the heat of last night. "That's all I wanted."

Closing my eyes, I swallow roughly. "One's all you're gonna get."

CHAPTER 13

DECLAN

"YOU'VE BEEN QUIET TODAY. What's going on?" Dad asks as he takes a seat next to me. Typically he would've been one of the first people I went to with what's on my mind, but for once I wanted to be the person who figured out shit on their own. Instead of being the kid who always goes to his Dad to help with all his problems, I want to be the adult who has the answers.

I'm changing the brake pads on one of our regulars. I have my air pods in, and usually that takes care of anyone wanting to talk to me too much. Today, it doesn't seem as if Dad's taking the hint. He stays in the seat and motions for me to take them out. I pretend like I mute them and take them out before standing to slip them in my pocket. "What'd you say?"

He looks at me like I'm an idiot. "Don't act like you can't hear me. Half the time you don't even have those son of a bitchin' things turned on, but I'll pretend like you did. You've been quiet today. What's going on?"

I sigh. "Girl shit."

"Translation: Claudia shit," he laughs, taking a drag off his cigarette. "If you were trying to hide whatever happened between the two of you a few days ago, you did a horrible job."

"Big words for a man who was supposed to quit smoking and only be using his vape a few times a day. I could blow your cover with mom."

He flicks at the hat on my head. "And I could tell her all the shit I covered for with you when you were a teenager, but we're both adults, Declan. I can handle my wife."

"Can you?" I grin, my eyebrows furrowing with the question. "She's coming down the stairs." I hitch my chin up to where my childhood home is connected to the shop.

He opens his mouth wide enough so the cigarette falls onto the floor, quickly snuffing it out with the toe of his boot, before turning around... where he sees no one. "You little fucker."

"Point proved, Dad. But I'll answer your question. You have experience with this shit – which I can't believe no one ever told me – not that I would ever think of Riley as anything other than my sister. But damn. Tell a guy."

"I really am sorry about that. It never came up, and your mom hated talking about her first husband. Riley was hurt every time his name was mentioned, and it was never a priority. I realize you should've been told, but I was trying to keep them from getting hurt. The situation you're in? You're fixing to figure out there's a lot of trauma to be had, which means it needs to be healed. Patience will be a virtue for you. You're going to have to prove yourself, even when you think you've done all you can do. Fuck, you'll think you've done it, that there's no more question in her mind that you're not like the fuck face who's hurt her, but there'll be a moment when she doubts." He shakes his head, as if remembering his own experiences.

"What do you do in those moments of doubt?" I take a drink of my coffee from earlier, which should be considered ice coffee at this point. The sounds of the shop fade into the background. Sometimes it's hard to hear yourself think when everyone's working at once, but not right now. I can make out every single word that comes out of his mouth.

"You keep going on," he shrugs. "Every time she's got a doubt, you continue to prove yourself to her. You're gonna stumble sometimes; no one can be perfect, and if she expects you to be, then maybe she's not the person for you. However, if you're consistent, she's going to know who you are."

I've never been the type to not believe in myself. Most would say I've got too much confidence most of the time. But this woman and her son? They deserve for the best, and I'm terrified I won't be able to give it to her. "What do you think I should do to start out?"

Dad smirks. "If there's one thing I *do* know about women, it's that they'll forget to take care of themselves to make sure their kids are taken care of. You wanna make a good impression? Text her, tell her you have her dinner planned out, or don't be that forceful with it and ask her instead. Either way, let her know you're thinking of not only her, but her son. That's important. If you end up falling in love with her, he's going to be a huge part of her life – for the rest of it."

I nod, reaching out to hug him. I lucked out in the dad department. "I appreciate you, I hope you know that."

"I do. Love you, kid," he says as he messes up my hair. "Go get that woman if she's who you want."

She is.

She's everything I want.

Pulling my phone out of my pocket, I use my thumb to unlock it and then take a seat, debating way too long on what I'm going to say to her. In the end, I go with the truth.

D: I had a really good time with you the other night. I'd like to take some of the pressure off of you… can I take you and Jay out for dinner?

My hands are sweating like I'm a whore in church as I wait for her to answer. When she does I look at it twice, just to make sure I've read it correctly.

C: I'd love that. Where do you wanna go?

CHAPTER 14
CLAUDIA

"ARE you sure you wanna do this?" Mom asks as I finish brushing Jay's hair, and then run a little lip gloss over my lipstick.

I roll my eyes before I turn back around to face her. "Do you not think I should? You've known Declan since he was a baby, just like I have. If there's anyone I trust with myself and my son, it's him. What are your reservations?"

She sits down, taking a drink of her sweet tea. Honestly 'tea' is being generous; it's mostly sugar. It's a wonder she doesn't have diabetes. "He sees you have a child, Claudia. Do you wonder if he thinks you're loose?"

"Oh give me a break! This isn't the eighteen-hundreds. We're in the two-thousands, Mom. Over half of the world is single moms at this point. Do you think that means all of them are whores who lie down and spread their legs for every man who comes up to them?"

"No," she's quick to answer.

"Then why do you think I am?"

This has been the crux of the issue since I had Jay. She's

treated me like I was sleeping with every man on the block. The truth of the matter is, Steven was my high school boyfriend. He was my first everything. I didn't let him sleep with me until I was twenty-three, because my mom scared me to death about having a child before I was married.

Paranoid didn't even begin to describe it. It took years for him to get a kiss. I never wanted to disappoint her, and I sure as fuck didn't want to end up in the same situation as her. I knew I would never hear the end of it. When I found out I was pregnant –although I was in my mid-twenties – I almost ran away. She loves Jay more than she ever imagined she would, this I know for certain, but when I told her I was pregnant, she cried.

She questioned me numerous times, asking if I knew what I was doing, what I was getting into, and if I realized how different my life would be from now on. It was unspoken, but she recommended I get an abortion.

I thought about it, but the moment I saw the positive pregnancy test, I loved the baby. I knew I could do all the things for him I'd wanted her to do for me. She hasn't answered my question, so I ask it again. "Why do you think I am?"

She sniffs. "I taught you better than to put yourself in the same situation I found myself in. When you did? It was a slap in the face to me; like you didn't take anything I said and retain it. As soon as you saw a dick you went for it, and now here I am, Claudia, stuck taking care of another baby when I should be enjoying my life."

Tears burn my eyes. She's *stuck*. I clear my throat. "I hope my son never thinks I'm stuck. I love him, and that's all there is to it."

Outside, I hear the rev of a motorcycle.

Without a doubt I know it's Declan.

"C'mon, Jay. You ready to go to dinner with Declan?"

"Dec? Yes!" he yells, clapping his hands.

"I'm assuming we're okay to come back after dinner, and it's okay for Declan to park his bike out there? We're taking my car."

"Claudia, that's not what I meant. You're welcome here, he's welcome here."

"Great, we'll be back later."

Grabbing Jay's bag, and him, we head outside.

"Hey," Dec smiles as he walks toward us. He's carrying a rose in one hand and a toy excavator in the other.

"Are those for us?" I paste a smile on my face.

"They are," he hands me the rose. "Are you okay? You seem a little upset."

"Just some irritation with my mom, nothing you need to worry about."

He bends down, getting to eye level with my son. "I saw this, and thought of you, Jay man. You like construction stuff, don't ya?"

Jay is shy. The only people who typically bring him things are me and Riley, so he buries his head in my leg. "He does. Tell him thank you, buddy."

Jay whispers, "Thank you."

"I'm glad you like it," Declan replies as he reaches out, running a hand along Jay's chin. It's affectionate, and something I've always wanted to see be done with my son. Steven isn't touchy-feely, and I can't remember the last time he actually touched either of us.

"I love it," he whispers excitedly.

The smile on his face is one of the best things I've ever seen. "C'mon, let's get you in your car seat so we can head to dinner."

"Want me to do it?" Declan asks.

"I got it. I've got it down to less than two minutes. The

quicker we can get him in there, the quicker we can get away from here."

He reaches out, grabbing my hand as I walk to the back of the car. "Later, when you can, will you tell me about it?"

I've never been the type to want to lay all my feelings and problems at someone else's feet. The truth of the matter is, no one's ever asked. This is all new to me, and I don't know how far I'm willing to trust him, but I've prayed for this. Late at night when I'm in bed and I allow the loneliness to creep in, let the tears fall, I've prayed for someone to take part of this from me; to have a partner, someone to carry part of this load.

But can I trust it?

Can I trust him?

I'll never know until I try. "I will. It'll probably scare you away, but I will."

He reaches over, palming my cheek. "You can try, but I promise, I'm a lot tougher than I look."

CHAPTER 15
DECLAN

THE LONELINESS and fear in her eyes is like a stab to the gut. The woman standing in front of me is so different from the girl I once knew, the one who would run around the apartment with Riley, tormenting me when they would spend the night together. It got on my fucking nerves back then, but now I miss it; the giggles as they would flush the toilet while I was in the shower, or put hot sauce where I couldn't see it.

They would run off cackling while I'd be stuck trying to get my shit under control. It used to get on my damn nerves, but right now? I miss it. Back then she had a glow about her, a bright smile that would light up the entire room. I haven't seen that version of her since well before she had Jay. Steven scooped her up and snuffed out her light. I wanna be the person who helps bring that glow back to her.

"Why are you so quiet?" she asks, sitting in the passenger seat of her car.

"Just thinking about how surreal it is, that I'm in this spot with you again. When I drove y'all to work the other night, I didn't think I'd be right back here in this seat driving all of us to dinner."

She shifts, almost nervously. "Are you having second thoughts?"

"Fuck no."

Jay makes a noise in the back. "Uh oh..."

Claudia laughs. "Yeah, he said a bad word, didn't he?"

"I didn't even think about it. I'm sorry." My cheeks heat as I realize how stupid of a mistake that was.

"It's okay, I let them slip sometimes. He repeats everything though, like a parrot. It's one of the first things you'll learn about him if you hang with him long enough."

"Oh, yeah?" I look at him in the rearview mirror. "You like embarrassing your mom?"

Jay laughs, "Fuck no."

I groan, closing my eyes, and shaking my head. "I deserve that."

"Hopefully that's all he'll say," she sighs. "The worst is when he does it in front of my mom. I try so hard to be the perfect mother for him and I know she's judging me already, so when he does stuff like that, it's awful."

"You don't have to be perfect." I reach over, grabbing her hand. "All you have to do is teach him right from wrong. He adores you."

She makes a non-committal noise in the back of her throat. "Where are you taking us, anyway?" She changes the subject so quickly I almost get whiplash.

"Figured I couldn't go wrong with pizza."

"Pizza! Pepperoni?" Jay questions from the backseat.

"If that's what you want, that's what we'll have."

She flashes an indulgent smile at me. "It's his favorite. Safe to say you picked something good."

Warmth expands in my chest. I didn't pick it because I

knew it was his favorite, I did it because I hoped it was something they'd enjoy. "I'm glad," I get into the turning lane and wait patiently for traffic to thin out. If this were just me, I'd have chanced it a few times, but with the two of them in the car, I wait until traffic is completely clear.

Pulling into a parking spot, I take it out of gear, and then turn the car off. Glancing over at her, I give her a smirk. "You ready?"

She smiles back. It's a real one, relaxed and comfortable. "Yeah, I am."

If I were alone, I'd pump my fist and do a fucking happy dance. There's a double meaning with these words. As if she's willing to give me a real chance. We get out and I hurry over to her side to help her get Jay out. When she puts him on the ground, he reaches up to hold my hand.

It's such an innocent gesture, and it hits me straight in the chest. For a kid who keeps getting disappointed by his dad, I can't believe he's willing to offer me that hand. We walk slowly, and when we enter, we're assaulted by the noise of a busy restaurant.

"Hey, Dec, take a seat wherever you want. I'll be there to take your order in just a sec," my favorite waitress, Mary, greets as she rushes past me in a blur. Her eyes widen as she sees I'm with someone. Her gaze goes down to where Jay is holding my hand. "Need a booster seat too?"

"Please."

"You come here often?"

"I'm a bachelor," I defend. "I can't expect my mom and sister to feed me all the time. Their pizzas are so big here, I can make one last at least two or three nights," I shrug.

Her gaze works its way down my body. "I wish I could look the way you do and eat out every single meal."

"I work out," I laugh. "More than I want to."

"Thanks," she quips, winking. "I truly do appreciate it. Those abs are the type people write romance novels about."

Licking my lips, I duck my head. "I'll remember that when I'm dying from doing a hundred sit-ups a night." It's getting hot in here between us, and I know if I don't stop it, we'll be in trouble. "Let's go get a table."

Together we move through the crowd of people. If she wondered whether or not I really do come here a lot, it's confirmed by the amount of people who wave and call out my name. Granted, a lot of them know me from the shop, but just as many know me because I come in here so often. I point to the back, where there's a booth.

The three of us slide in, her sitting next to Jay, me on my side by myself. Menus are tucked behind the napkin holder, so I grab one and hand it to her.

"You already know what you're getting, right?"

"Pepperoni pizza, right my man?" I ask as I look over at Jay. He nods before grabbing a crayon that sits beside the napkin holder. There are big swatches of craft paper on the table, which is one of the reasons I came here. He can draw to his heart's content and not worry about messing anything up. He starts doodling, and when he seems content, I turn my attention to Claudia.

"What's good here?" she asks, "if I don't want pizza? I have it every other night with this one," she admits, hooking a thumb over at Jay.

"The chicken parm is amazing, the spaghetti is an old family recipe, and their hot subs are really good too. I've eaten everything on this menu – except for the eggplant parm."

"Not your thing?" She laughs when I wrinkle my nose and shake my head quickly.

"Not at all. My mom used to try to make me eat it when I was a kid."

"Riley loves it," she giggles.

"I'm aware." My voice is deadpan. "Whenever I wouldn't eat it, mom would be like, 'well, at least one of my kids likes when I slave over a decent meal for them.' Busted my balls every time," I chuckle.

"Your mom is sweet."

"She is, unless you cross her. Then she's a hellcat that even my dad doesn't want to deal with."

"You've been on the receiving end of that, I take it?" She tilts her cup, sipping some of her water. The way her throat moves against the liquid makes me wonder what it would be like if she took my cock down that way.

Adjusting in the booth, I answer the question. "More often than I meant to, that's for sure."

"Hey, Dec, who are your friends?" Mary asks as she comes over, pad and pen in hand.

"This beautiful lady is Claudia, and this handsome kid is Jay."

She smiles at both of them. "That they are. What can I get for all of you?"

We order, and when she's gone, Claudia leans back against the booth, her gaze flickering over to where Jay is coloring. "This is a nice place. When you texted me, I wasn't sure I was going to say yes."

"I know." I take a drink of the one beer I'm allowing myself tonight.

"I didn't think I hesitated that badly."

"You didn't," I assure her. "But I know how much you care for him and don't want him to get hurt," I admit, tilting my head over at Jay. "I don't wanna make promises I can't keep, because we don't know how things will end up. None of us do, and we don't know the future, but I can promise you I will never do anything to purposely make you think less of me. I want to be a part of his life, be a part of your life. I know the two of you are a packaged deal, okay?"

She nods. "That's the nicest thing anybody's ever said to me."

"I'm glad, but, sweet girl, that's fuckin' sad. You deserve the world, and I'm gonna give it to you."

CHAPTER 16
CLAUDIA

C: I'm too old to hang.

D: LOL! What do you mean?

C: Staying out with you on a Wednesday night before I have school in the morning? I'll have to think about it before I do it again. I'm exhausted.

D: You want me to DoorDash you some coffee?

GOD, this guy... Like where was he when I decided to swear off men because the last one I got off a dating app was a fucking perv with a MILF complex?

C: That's sweet of you, but I'm going to stop and get one before I drop Jay off at daycare. Thanks for inviting us out last night. I don't know if I thanked you, but we had a really good time.

D: I did too, and I thought your mom watched Jay?

C: She does when I've worked the night before. That way he doesn't have to spend so much time at daycare, but when I'm off, I send him to traditional daycare the next day. He gets to be with other kids and they teach him his ABC's, numbers, etc. That's work my mom doesn't do with him.

D: Gotcha. I hope you have a good day.

C: You too.

The smile on my face would be contagious if anyone else could see it. But mom's already left.

The days she doesn't have Jay, she treats as almost vacations. She's gone before we even wake up – heaven forbid I ask her to help us get ready – and she doesn't come home until we're in bed for the night. I've really got to find a way to afford an apartment on my own.

Luckily I'm in my last semester of college, and I'm hopeful I'll be able to transfer at the hospital. Instead of doing registration, I've put in applications in the accounting and payroll departments, since that's what my degree will be in. I'm waiting to hear back, but I hope I can stay there. If I can, I should be able to get an apartment for us within the first couple of months after graduation.

Jay needs his own space, and so do I.

"Jay, come get your stuff. We gotta go!" I yell as I walk through the apartment, turning off lights and straightening up.

He toddles in, grabbing his backpack and lunchbox. "What's for lunch?" he asks, sounding far too old for a three-year-old.

"Chicken noodle soup, and you've got some strawberries in there too."

The smile on his face is all the reward I need. I'd stayed up late after we got home to cut up the strawberries, so I wouldn't have to do it this morning. "Thanks, Mommy," he says as he leans in, hugging my leg.

"Anything for you, Jay man."

Funny how I hadn't known what those words meant until I had this little boy who makes my world spin round.

———

"SIX WEEKS," the professor is saying as she stands in front of the class. "Six weeks until your final, and I'm worried that some of you aren't going to make it."

Typically I would be scared at the way he's talking. Immediately I would wonder if I was one of those people, but in this class, I know I'm not. I've worked hard to understand the tax laws, and I've taken it as seriously as I take being a mother to my son.

"Can we do extra credit?" someone yells out.

"No. If the IRS comes to one of your clients saying you did something wrong, do you think they're going to say 'well here's some extra credit'? You have to learn this. I suggest you get someone in the class who knows what they're doing to tutor you, or you need to study harder."

There's a loud groan that travels through the room.

"I'm serious," she says. "If you don't understand these key elements, you aren't going to pass the class. That's it for today."

As we gather up our things, everyone is complaining. She calls my name, motioning for me to come up to her desk.

"Yes, ma'am?"

"You know what you're doing; you get it better than anyone

else in this class right now. If anyone comes to you, you ask for money for tutoring. Don't you offer it for free," she advises.

I laugh. "Trust me, I don't have time to tutor anyone, much less offer it for free."

"Good. You're going places, Claudia. I can't wait to see what you do once you get out of here."

"From you're lips to God's ears, Professor."

As I walk out, even the coldness of the day isn't enough to bring me down. My head is held high, and I'm grateful for all the chances I've been given.

CHAPTER 17
DECLAN

"WHY ARE YOU MONOPOLIZING MY FRIEND?" Riley asks as she comes sauntering into the shop, hands on her hips, lips pursed.

I'm not in the mood to listen to my sister, but she's not going to let me hear the end of this. "What do you mean?"

"Don't play dumb with me. Every time I text Claudia lately, she's either with you, she's working, or doing homework."

"Don't hate; because she's got something happening that's not you," I tease her, waiting for the response.

She pops me upside the head.

"What the fuck was that for?"

"It's a reminder." She points her finger at me, like she's my mother. "That's my best friend. She's been hurt before, by too many people, and if you end up being one of them, I will never forgive you."

I knew this was coming, honestly I've been waiting for it. What kind of a best friend would Riley be if she didn't ask me these questions, if she didn't stand up for her friend? Even if she is my sister.

"Riley, it's not like I need you breathing down my damn neck. Don't you think I know what I'm getting into?" I've thought about it way more than I should replaying every damn scenario through my head about how we might end up, trying to be careful at every turn.

"No!" she screams, huffing so hard it pushes her bangs up off her forehead. "I don't. I think you have really good intentions, but you have no idea what could happen if you fuck it up."

"I think I do." I don't yell back at her, but my tone is stern. "I'd appreciate it if you'd let me live my life. You have no idea..."

"Hey, you two," Mom yells from where she stands on the landing of the stairs. "Why don't you take it down a notch and come up here?"

"Good job." I throw my wrench onto the workbench, and follow my sister upstairs.

When we get there, Mom is sitting at the kitchen table, and she's got two cups already placed down for us. "Have a seat."

I throw a glare over at Riley. "This is your fault."

"It's yours," she mumbles.

"I thought I told you both to have a seat," Mom says firmly, pointing at the two empty chairs.

I can't remember the last time she talked to us like this, as if we're little kids. It's embarrassing, especially since I'm trying to prove I'm mature enough to care for an older woman and her child. Pulling out the chair, I flop down, crossing my arms over my chest.

Once I do this, Riley does the same, although she adds a sigh.

"What the hell is wrong with you two?" Mom asks, after we've sat in a tense silence for way too long.

"She's in my business," I start.

Riley tries to talk over me. "He's going to hurt Claudia and Jay."

"How do you know?" I roar. "See? This is what pisses me off!"

"Stop!" Mom whistles, bringing our arguments to a halt. "We raised both of you to respect each other way more than what you're doing right now. I want you to talk one at a time, and I want you to listen to what the other is saying. We're not leaving this table until y'all can act like you have some sense again. Riley, you go first."

Of course.

"Claudia and Jay have all but been abandoned by Steven," she says, picking at the polish on her nails. "I know him," she points over at me, "he's never had a serious relationship, and this is gonna be his first one? I mean, give me a break."

"That's not fair," I grit out, and cross my arms over my chest.

"No, it's not," Mom interjects. "When your dad and I got together, he'd never been in a serious relationship before. Do you think I should've blown him off because of that?" she challenges Hadley.

"No, of course not, but he was older."

"My age has nothing to do with this. I've had a crush on her since I knew what that meant. I just kept it to myself. I'm sorry you were born before me, and have the advantage of being older. Name one other person you know my age who is about to be responsible for a business... Someone who's going to be taking care of their entire family. Respectfully, Riley, fuck you if you don't think any better of me than that."

"While I wouldn't have said that, at least we're starting to get to the heart of the matter." Mom puts a hand out to me, grasping hold of mine. "Now, Riley, what exactly is your issue?"

"Her whole life is her son, and she's given up everything to take care of him. I can't tell you the last time the two of us even went out for a girl's night."

"Is that what this is?" I interrupt her. "You're jealous because I'm getting more of her time than you are?"

"She's been my best friend since we were kids," she defends.

"But you're not offering her the chance to be her partner, and you're not going to. She's not a lesbian, and neither are you. You can be her best friend, but you can't be her partner, Riley. I want to be that person. I'm willing to do whatever it takes to prove to her I want to be a part of her life. If that makes me seem like a liar, then so be it."

"The only way you're going to be able to prove that is if you prove it," she says, leaning over the table in my direction. "And if you hurt her or Jay, you'll have to answer to me."

Holding my hands up, I nod. "Understood. But if you stand in my way, you'll have to answer to me. Understand?"

She nods. "I won't stand in your way, but I will fuck you up if you fuck this up."

"Same goes, Sis."

Mom huffs, pushing back from the table. "I expect the two of you to treat not only yourselves with respect, but Claudia and Jay too. They're just trying to live their lives. I'm sure neither one of them thought they'd get in the middle of a sibling rivalry. Be nice."

Riley and I nod before getting up and walking out of the apartment using different exits. I've never felt more certain about anything than I do about being a part of this single mother and her son's life.

CHAPTER 18
CLAUDIA

"WHY HAVE YOU BEEN IGNORING ME?"

My head pops up from where I'm entrenched in home-work. This is my quiet place, and I should've known Riley would know exactly where to find me. "I haven't been ignoring you," I laugh as I move my stuff out of the way so she has a place to sit down. "I've just been really busy."

"With my brother, huh?"

I sigh, taking a sip of my iced coffee. "Not only with him, but with school, work, and taking care of Jay, I'm swamped. What little bit of free time I do have, I've been spending with him. I didn't mean for it to happen, Riles. One day I was doing everything on my own, the next there was someone who was interested in helping me, who didn't care what I could give them in return. " I don't know why I feel the need to explain myself to her. Maybe it's because she's my best friend, or maybe it's because I'm still not exactly sure what's going on between Declan and I. Either way, I'm offering way more to her than I've even offered to myself.

"Really? I know you've wanted someone to share your life with, someone who could be a father for Jay."

"That's not what this is," I hurry to continue the explanation. "I didn't expect him..."

"What the hell is that supposed to mean? I'm trying to figure out what's going on. This is my little brother, Claud."

Putting my forehead in my palm, I try to collect my thoughts. Right now they seem to be twirling around in a tornado of possibilities and different versions of the truth. "I know, trust me, I know." Tears flood my eyes. "I've warned myself about that. He's young, and he's got his whole life ahead of him. I've asked myself over and over why he might want to be tied down to me and Jay. Maybe he's a glutton for punishment?" I let a watery giggle escape before wiping at the tears pooling under my eyes.

She sighs. "He's not. He and I got into an argument about you yesterday."

"What? No! I don't wanna cause issues between the two of you."

"It wasn't you," she mumbles, playing with a piece of paper. "It was me. I had to ask. I had to make sure he has yours and Jay's best interest at heart. Nothing would hurt me more than knowing my own family screwed over someone I care about."

There's a sickening feeling in the pit of my stomach, but I have to ask. "And what do you think now that you've questioned him?"

She smiles softly, a happiness covering her face I haven't seen in a long time. If I've had issues in the love department, Riley has blown the fucking department up. "I think for the first time in his life, my little brother is totally in love, although he doesn't know it yet. He cares for you a lot, Claudia. He's everything I would've wanted for you before Steven, and now he's everything I do want for you after Steven. It's going to be hard for me," she admits, sniffling slightly, "letting you go as a best friend, because I know once you get to know Dec, really get to know him, you're going to fall in love with him. It's hard not to. He's a really fucking good guy, and his whole life he's wanted a relationship. Whether he knew it or not, he's the type of person who's needed to be monogamous since he was a teenager. If you're the person he's picked, then I'm fucking stoked for the both of you. Just give me time to get used to it."

Tears are now streaming down my face in a way I never imagined they would. My best friend, the person I've trusted with everything since we met each other, has put everything into perspective for me. Finally, I'm allowing someone else to be in my life, to be in Jay's. "This is hard for me..."

"I know it is, and I'm happy for you. I'm gonna miss you, because our friendship won't be the same. You and I both know when women find their people, friends go by the wayside."

"Oh shut the fuck up, Riley. He's your brother. I'll see you almost as much as I see him. You'll be there, right?"

"Whenever you need me, I'll always be there, but I know I won't be your first call anymore."

"That's a lie," I giggle. "I don't know when I'll feel comfortable calling him first. You know as well as I do that it takes me a while to depend on others."

She smirks. "If there's anyone you can depend on, it's him. As much as I like to think of him as the little boy who had my heart from the moment my mom had him, he's now a grown man. He's someone I can't protect. I have to allow him to make his own decisions; even if I'm worried those decisions will end up hurting him. It's time I allow him to be the man he's grown into. It's hard, but I'm going to step back."

"No matter what, I'm always going to need you, but you're right. I've waited a long time to be able to share my life with someone else. I want to give a stable life to Jay. I don't want his experience to be what mine's been. Everyone always said you want more for your kids, and I understand what that means. What if I fail him?" I put words to my worst fear.

"You're not going to," she shakes her head, a bewildered smile on her face. "Everything you've done is for him. There's no way you're going to lose what you've worked so hard for. With Declan by your side, and our family behind you, you've more than got this, Claudia."

I blow out a breath. "I know. It's just nerve wracking to put all my eggs in one basket. I don't assume it's all going to work out; I try to plan for every single contingency."

"For once in your life, girl, let it be. It'll work out, but you've gotta trust the process."

Trust the process?

Here goes nothin'.

CHAPTER 19
DECLAN

IT'S BEEN A FUCKING long day. Everything that could go wrong has. From the wrong parts being delivered, to the lunch I ordered being a vegetarian option, which I've never ordered in my life. It all feels fucking *off*.

"You ever have a day when you just want to close up shop and say see y'all later?" I ask dad, as I throw away my twenty-dollar lunch.

"At least once a week for the last thirty years," he laughs. "What's going on today?"

He's been out for most of the day, trying to get some help with some parts we haven't been able to get lately because of some supply chain issues, so he hasn't been here for all of the shit I've had to deal with.

"Everything that can go wrong has, including getting a goddamn vegetarian meal. I mean, when have I ever? This is a place I order from all the damn time, too."

"Why don't you take the afternoon off? I've asked a lot of you since you expressed interest in taking over the business. Part of being the boss is knowing you can take a random afternoon off in the middle of the week. Why don't you do that right now?"

I sigh heavily. "This oil needs to be changed, and those brakes need to be checked," I say, pointing over to another bike.

"And I can do all of that, probably even faster than you can. I've been at this job longer than you, in case you forgot. Go, enjoy the afternoon. It's cold, but at least the sun's out. Go spend some time not here."

"Alright, I'll see y'all tomorrow."

As I walk out, I grab my jacket and head out to where my own motorcycle is parked. It takes me a few minutes, but I bundle up against the wind and cold temperatures. When I have myself as protected as I'm gonna get, I start the bike, put it in gear, and get the hell away from all of my problems.

This is my favorite place to be; has been since I got my first bike at fifteen. I was one of three kids who rode their motorcycles in high school. In fact, I've never owned a regular vehicle. It's always been something of a badge of honor for me, but maybe it's time for me to grow up, especially with Claudia and Jay hopefully becoming a permanent part of my life.

The void of thoughts when I hear the wind whipping past my helmet is what I love most about riding. Today though, those thoughts are rising up, and they're all coming back to Claudia and Jay.

I need to see her.

As I cross the bridge, heading into the urban renewal portion of the city, I spot a taco truck, and thoughts of that wasted vegetarian meal come back with a vengeance. My stomach growls and clenches hard.

Mind made up, I pull into the parking lot, hop off my bike, and walk right up to the truck.

"What can I get for you, my man?"

"Dude, the biggest fuckin' meal you got. I'm starving."

He laughs, a smile across his face. "I got ya. Anything you don't like?"

"Not a huge fan of cilantro, it tastes like soap, but besides that, no. Hit me with what ya have."

"Give me about fifteen minutes."

Over to the side, there's a pavilion. I distinctly remember my mom bringing me and my sister here in the summer when we became too much to handle in the apartment. She'd bring our lunch, we'd play in the fountain, and then we'd eat under the covered pavilion.

This must be what people mean when they talk about core memories, because I haven't thought about it in years.

Pulling my phone out of my pocket, I shoot off a text to Claudia.

It's a long shot, and I want it more than I should, but I do it anyway.

D: Today's been a shit day. Spend the afternoon and night with me? I understand if you can't, but I would love it if you can.

CHAPTER 20
CLAUDIA

THE TEXT from Declan is burning a hole in my pocket where it sits on my phone. This isn't me, but my mind goes back to what Riley said.

Trust the process.

I want to be with him, without anyone interrupting us or anyone even knowing where I am. He's my little secret right now. I have to share so much with the world around me.

My time with Jay.

My money with my mom.

My life with everyone who needs a piece of me.

Puffing out a breath, I pick up my phone and place a call, knowing I'm going to be lying through my teeth, but at the same time, knowing it's necessary.

"Hey, Mom," I start when she answers. "Do you think you could watch Jay tonight? The hospital called and asked if I could take an extra shift, and you know I need the money."

"Why can't he go to daycare?" she questions almost immediately.

"It's full for the night." This happens sometimes, but they

always make room for him if I pick up an extra shift. She, on the other hand, doesn't have to know that. "There are only so many cribs, and you know I usually reserve his spot as soon as my schedule is posted. I understand if you can't."

"Typically I would say no, but I have no plans."

I don't give her a chance to say anything. "Thank you so much, I'll see you both in the morning." I hang up like the phone is on fire, with the brightest smile on my face, and the lightest my heart has felt since before I had Jay.

> C: Where are you?

> D: The Urban Renewal Area across the bridge. I'm eating lunch in the pavilion.

> C: I know exactly where that is. I'll be right there.

Getting to my car and making it off campus takes forever. It seems as if every red light catches me, and everyone in front of me is going slow in the fast lane. In reality, it only takes twenty minutes to make it to where Declan is. Immediately I see his bike parked over to the side, by itself. I take the spot next to him, make sure everything is off, bundle up, and then head out into the cold.

The wind is freezing coming off the river, but it's so quiet here, I don't even mind. It causes my eyes to water, but I blink it away as quickly as I can. "Hey," I wave as I get closer.

He waves right back, getting up to come meet me. "I wasn't sure what you would say when I sent that message. Thanks for agreeing."

We hold hands as we walk toward the picnic tables. "Thanks for inviting me. I have to be honest, I wasn't sure I should accept, but not only have I not had many offers the last few years; none of those offers have been as hot as you."

He ducks his head down, and when he lifts it back up, his cheeks are red – not with the burn of cold, but with the heat of embarrassment. "You're making me blush," he laughs.

"You're the only person I've ever made blush," I laugh along with him.

There are heaters in the pavilion and while I'm not freezing, it's still quite cold. Shivering, I bundle further into my jacket.

"You wanna get outta here?" he asks, hitching his chin toward where our vehicles are.

"Where are we gonna go?"

"My apartment. There's a back entrance. No one has to know we're there."

What he's suggesting sounds amazing. There are so many demands made on my time every day, I don't get anything that's just mine. "Let's do it," I nod, excitement welling up in my stomach.

He grabs my hand and together we run for the parking lot, as if we have this great secret between us. The feeling of giddiness bubbles up in my throat, causing me to giggle. Declan laughs too, although his is deep and full of a sexy promise that I'm not sure I want to acknowledge.

Once we get to my car, he turns me around so my back is pressed against the driver's side door. His hand rests gently on the side of my face. "I'll be right behind you, but I want you to know something. If you don't want to pull into the back alley and go to my apartment, you don't have to. I'm not interested in making you do anything you don't want to. This is completely up to you, sweet girl."

I swallow roughly, nodding. "I get that, and I thank you for it. Decisions are things I have to make constantly."

"Yeah, but I think we both know options are new for you. A lot of the decisions you make are because you have to, not because you want to. And when I say that, don't think I mean it as a pity thing. That's not it at all. I think it's important for me to show you I know how hard this is for you, and to understand what you're sacrificing to spend the afternoon with me."

The truth of what he says hits me right in the chest. For longer than I care to admit, no one's thought about what I've sacrificed to be where I am. Even if every day I feel as if I'm falling further and further behind everyone else my age, I'm still proud of how far I've come. Every bit of progress I've made, I've earned. "Thank you, Dec. I don't think many people have tried to understand where I'm coming from, or realize how hard life has been."

He tucks a piece of hair behind my ear. "I see you, Claud. No matter how hard you try to hide yourself, I see you."

CHAPTER 21
DECLAN

FOLLOWING Claudia back to my apartment, I try to stay at a respectable distance, but I'm nervous as fuck that she'll drive right past the turnoff and go home. Until faced with the thought of her choosing to not stay with me, the nerves didn't start, but they're here in full force now.

We come to the intersection that leads to the alley of our buildings. My hands shiver inside my gloves, and I promise myself it won't be the end of the world if she chooses not to.

When her turn signal pops on, I let go of the largest breath I've ever held. I follow her in, and park next to her. She's slow getting out, but when she does, she reaches over and grasps my hand in hers. "Let's go."

Together we climb the steps and then enter. When I shut the door, it's as if I'm shutting out the rest of the world.

It's awkward as we look at each other. "I've never really hung out with a girl before," I admit, laughing to cover up how out of my element I am.

"The only other guy I've hung out with is Steven, and we always did what he wanted to do," she admits.

"What do you want to do?" I ask, hoping she'll give some direction to us both. "If this was your perfect day, what would it be?"

She sighs, settling into the reality of this situation. "I'd change into some comfortable clothes, spend the afternoon on the couch watching something that isn't a cartoon, I'd order dinner, and then sleep without having to worry if I'm going to be woken up by a toddler who still isn't potty trained yet."

"Then that's exactly what we'll do," I promise.

"I don't even have any clothes to change into," she reminds me.

"I can take care of that." Leading her to my bedroom, I come to a stop in front of my dresser, opening the door that houses all my sweatpants and t-shirts. "Take your pick."

"Are you serious?" Her tone is bemused, as if no one has ever let her do something like this before.

"Yeah, the hottest thing I'll probably ever see is you wearing my clothes, sweet girl. Give me a memory that'll last when we have to get back to reality."

Her gaze heats as if she seems to realize this is different; we're different with each other than we are with anyone else. She's letting her guard down, and I'm letting myself be vulnerable.

"I'm gonna go change," she heads for the bathroom.

"I'll do the same. Meet you out there on the couch?"

She nods, rolling her lips together. "Hey Dec?"

"Yeah?"

"Thank you for this."

"You never have to thank me."

"I do, but I appreciate you for making me feel like I don't have to."

Watching her leave, I shake my head. This woman is every-thing, and the fact no one's ever made her a priority before infuriates me. But she's willing to give me the next fifteen or so hours, and I'm going to make them the best they can be.

I'M ALREADY SITTING THERE when she comes out, covered up with a blanket. I hold the remote up. "It's yours. You can decide what we're watching this afternoon."

She smiles, laughing slightly. "I don't even know what's on TV other than cartoons."

"Lucky for you, I have just about every streaming service and cable. Chances are, you can watch whatever you want."

Claud holds the remote like it's something precious; the same way I'd like to be holding her. She clicks through the TV, going from one streaming service to another. Just when it appears she's made a decision, she moves onto something else.

"Am I getting on your nerves with my indecision?"

"Not at all. This is about you, not me," I assure her.

"This is one of my favorites," she lands on a movie I've seen a few times.

"Really? This one?" I glance over at her, my eyebrow raised in surprise.

"I like to laugh just like everybody else," she defends. "It's the guy with the infected tongue ring for me, and the guy who has narcolepsy who falls asleep at the most inopportune times of the race."

I laugh thinking about those parts of the movie. "Nah, it's the girl pilot who terrorizes her cheating boyfriend and destroys his truck, for me."

She laughs back. "Or the referee. Face it, Rat Race is a classic."

"That it is," I agree.

Getting comfortable, we settle in for a nice long afternoon.

CHAPTER 22
CLAUDIA

"THERE IS no way that's you," I crack up as I lay on the couch next to him, looking at pictures on his phone.

"It is," he sighs. "Mom likes to post it on every throwback Thursday, or on my birthday when she's feeling feisty. I get so annoyed when she does, because everyone always comments about how cute I look in my Spiderman undies."

"Oh c'mon, you know you're cute," I reach out, tapping his nose.

"I wouldn't say I know it, it's nice to hear it every once in a while." He grabs hold of my finger, dragging me closer to him.

I'm taken off balance, and fall against him harder than I mean to. Our gazes connect and it's as if the world stops turning and we're the only two people in that orbit. His palm cups my cheek, before running down to my neck. The heat of his touch is enough to burn straight through me. It's the type of passion everyone wants to feel at least once in their life. If this is my one chance, I'm going to hold onto it with both hands and never let it go.

Slowly, we lean toward each other, our lips touching.

This kiss is the kind that promises a slow fuck against a wall in the pouring rain. Not that I've ever had that, but I want.

I want it all with Declan.

My arms wrap around his neck, pulling us closer together. My legs hook around his waist, wanting to feel every inch of him against me. Smearing his lips down my throat, I groan loudly as he latches onto the tender flesh, sucking fiercely. The answering ache between my thighs is a fire only he can quench.

I grip his t-shirt in between my fingers, yanking against the cotton.

"Goddamn, I love you wearing my clothes," he moves his hands to my waist, pushing his big shirt up past my bra and over my head. "Knowing you have this lacy shit under there, and you letting me be the one to see it. That's special and gets me hard as hell."

He rubs his length against me, and it makes the ache worse. "I want you," I whisper.

He pulls back, eyes dark, face heated. "You don't have to whisper. There's no one here but us. You can be as loud as you want, while I make you come."

"I don't know how loud I'll be, but thanks for the reminder I don't have any other ears around here." Grasping my fingers into his hair, I pull him down to the bare skin above the lace of my bra.

"You want me there?" He asks, tilting his head up.

"Please..."

"Here?" He asks slightly off of where I want him to be. Suddenly I understand he's being playful.

"Too cold."

"Here?" He questions, moving his mouth other.

"Warmer."

With sure fingers, he pulls the material down, positioning

his lips over my nipple. It's so tight, it's begging to meet him in the middle. "Here?"

His breath is hot against my skin. "Scorching. Put me outta my misery."

"With pleasure."

Those words are the gateway to what I know is going to be an obsession with the man hovering over me. In this moment, he stops being my best friends brother, and becomes the one I'll either want forever or judge everyone else against.

I'm engulfed in his heat, clinging to him like he's the lifeboat in the middle of a raging sea. Only this sea is my raging hormones.

His hands go up, gripping the arm of the couch. Using that leverage, he plants his knees on either side of my hips and propels his body into a standing position. Before I know what's happening, he's gathered me up in his arms, and we're heading toward his bedroom.

"I'm way too heavy," I argue.

"The fuck you are. I'm carrying my dreams in these arms. Ain't no other way I'd wanna go out."

I don't know what I did to deserve him, or how long I'm going to be able to hold onto it, but I'm going to hang on with both hands and dare someone to take him from me.

He lays me down on the bed, before hovering over me again. Never in my life have I felt so small, but so wanted at the same time.

"What do you want, sweet girl?"

"Not to make a decision, I do that every day in my life. I'm always the responsible one. Take that out of my hands, and show me what trusting my partner is like."

"You sure about this?"

"I am," I swallow roughly. "Take me away, Dec."

"Hold on tight, I'm gonna make you fly."

CHAPTER 23
DECLAN

SOMEHOW WE BOTH got out of our clothes without me noticing. Our bodies grind against one another. A groan is ripped out of my throat as her hand moves between us, gripping my cock tightly. "Fuck, Claudia."

"Fuck Claudia, that's what you should do. It's been way too long."

I chuckle, strained as it is. "I thought you said you wanted me to take the decisions away from you."

"I do, but you're taking too long."

Grabbing her hands, I pull them up over her head, holding her wrists in one hand. "These stay up here, and I'll make sure you have a damn good time."

She nods, a bemused smile on her face.

Moving down her body, I press her thighs apart, settling myself right where I want to be. Suctioning my mouth to her core, I put my tongue to work. Judging by the way she's squirming and panting, I'm doing something right.

The arms about her head move. One comes down to palm the back of my skull, pushing me deeper into her. Lifting my eyes so I can watch her face, I notice her other hand comes down to cup her breast, worrying her nipple in between her thumb and forefinger. Her hips lift against my tongue so hard, it's almost enough to push me off of her.

Reaching around behind her, I grip her ass in my hands, before hooking my arms around her thighs and pressing my thumbs on the outside of her pussy, holding her open to my mouth.

"Dec, Jesus Christ," she moans loudly. "Get inside me."

I slowly stop lapping at her clit, before pulling my mouth back. "Are you sure? It's been a while, according to you."

"And you're," she reaches down to grasp my cock again. "Bigger than what I had before. Just go slow."

She reaches out to grab the sheets, using them to push herself up against the pillows while I scoot up on my knees. Reaching over to the bedside table, I grab a condom before sitting back on my knees and suiting up.

Her eyes are hot as they stare at me, her lips roll together as she waits. I place my hand on her pubic bone, using my tongue to worry her clit, feeling the wetness drop down onto the pad of my thumb.

Holding the base of my cock, I slowly press into her, before I feel the resistance. She inhales deeply. "Slower?" I question.

"No, just give me a minute."

It takes everything I have not to move, but when she nods slightly, I do so. It's like coming home as I thrust fully into her. "Fuck you're hot," the words slip out of my mouth. I've always been the guy to wax poetic when sex is thrown into the mix. I'm bound to tell her I love her if I'm not careful.

"And you're hard, so hard. It feels so good," she tilts her head back against the pillows. "Don't hold back, Dec. Take me. Take me and show me what I've been missing."

This is what I've been waiting for. The okay to move

against her the way I need to. I stop measuring my thrusts and give my body over to what it wants.

We're pressing the bed frame against the wall, causing it to squeak as we push ourselves toward the precipice of the most passionate orgasm I've had.

Leaning down, I press my forehead against Claudia's, looking into her eyes as she reaches for the climax just out of both our reaches.

My knees are screaming, but I refuse to stop until she gets hers, and I get mine.

Her hands wrap around my shoulders, nails digging into my skin. I'll wear whatever she leaves there as badges of honor.

She tightens around me, and as she screams into the silence of the apartment, I groan along with her, and realize as I empty into the condom my life has just tilted on its axis.

It will never be the same again.

CHAPTER 24
CLAUDIA

"IS this what people do after they have one of, if not *the* best sexual experience of their lives?" I giggle as we sit outside on the fire escape.

We're bundled up against the freezing temperatures, and staying as close to the open window as possible. He grins over at me, cigarette dangling from his lips.

"Yeah, I guess sometimes ya just gotta have a smoke."

Watching him light it had been an exercise in futility. I never knew how hot it would be to watch a man light a match, cup his hand around the end of the cigarette, and then press the match to it. He'd inhaled deeply, taking a few tentative breaths before pulling it from his mouth and letting the tip glow a healthy orange.

"Can I try?" I ask shyly. I've never wanted to try before, but he makes it look sexy, cool, and forbidden.

"Yeah," he pulls it out with the pads of his thumb and forefinger, handing it over to me. "Inhale slowly, you will cough."

Bringing it up to my mouth, I hesitantly put it between my lips and take a steady breath. The taste is something I wasn't prepared for, but as it washes over me, I start to relax even more than I have since I got here. The remaining tension from my neck and back dissolves. "I can see why people get addicted to these."

'Yeah, I started smoking really young. Now I only have a real cigarette every now and then. Today though? It called for one."

"I agree," I giggle. "It calls for a drink too."

"Let me finish this and we can go in and get one."

I watch as he quickly finishes the stick of tobacco. It's gotten dark as we laid around in bed. The last time I did that was before Jay was born. If I remember correctly, it was when I was pregnant. I'd been upset because Steven and I weren't getting along. He'd offered me money to have an abortion, but being a mother is something I've always wanted.

It all hadn't happened the way I imagined it would, but it had happened, and I wasn't about to punish him for decisions I'd made.

Declan leans over, opening the window, ushering me through it. I stomp my feet, trying to get a little feeling back in them.

"I don't have a ton of food here," he says as he walks behind me. "But I do have frozen pizza and mozzarella sticks. It's my go-to meal when I don't want to order, or really cook."

"Mine is chicken nuggets and mac and cheese," I snort.

"There's no one here to judge us, we can eat our fancy as fuck pizza with a bottle of Jack and no one can say anything to us."

"Fancy as fuck pizza. I'll have to remember that."

He raises an eyebrow, grabbing the pizza out of the freezer. "I even have a pizza stone for the occasion."

"Look at you..."

"See," he shrugs. "Fancy as fuck."

While he puts everything in the oven, I have a seat at the island. "Do me a favor, Declan."

"Yeah," he turns around.

"Promise me we'll have more nights like this."

His face turns serious, as well as his tone. "If I thought you'd be receptive to it, I'd promise you the rest of our lives, sweet girl."

And in this moment, I hope those words are a premonition to what may be our future.

CHAPTER 25
DECLAN

TALK about crashing back into real life. Two days after we spent the afternoon together, she's called me, and I'm unsure of how to get her to calm down.

Claudia's voice on the other end of the phone is beyond panicked. "I've tried getting a hold of everybody, including Riley, but she's stuck at work. I can't leave, otherwise I'll lose this job..."

"Calm down, sweet girl. What is it you need?"

She takes a deep breath, exhaling slowly. "I need someone to go pick up Jay, and drop him off here."

"Okay, okay. I can do that."

"How? You don't have a car seat, you don't even have a car. You drive a motorcycle."

She's spiraling and I have to figure out a way to calm her down. "I could drive a fucking clown car and it wouldn't make a difference."

Immediately she stops talking. "What are you talking about?"

"It doesn't matter. It got you to stop freaking out, didn't it? Now can we have a real conversation?"

In the span of a few moments, the vibes over the phone change. She seems to compose herself with a deep breath. "Okay, Steven was supposed to pick up Jay for me at his other daycare. They just called me and said he's still there. They closed an hour ago. I took an early double, so I need someone to pick him up and bring him here."

"As I was saying earlier, I can take care of it for you. I'll borrow one of my parents' cars and go get him."

"What about the car seat?" She continues.

"There's a fucking Walmart on the way. Tell me what type of car seat you use for him and I'll get one."

"No, I can't ask you to waste that much money..."

"You also can't tell how to spend my money," I interrupt her. "And it's not a waste. I plan on having y'all in my life much longer than he'll have to be in that car seat." She's quiet for longer than I like. "Claud, I hope I didn't overstep a boundary."

"You, you didn't," she sniffles.

"Fuck I didn't mean to make you cry."

"It's just, no one has ever gone out of their way like this to help us, and you care, Declan. You really do care."

It feels as if I'm beating my head against the wall, but I know she needs this reassurance. The self-doubt with her has been ingrained because of situations she's had to deal with on her own.

Just like this one. But as my Dad told me when I asked his advice, I have to be there for her. That's what she needs more than anything. Me to be there and not make excuses.

"I do," my tone is serious, making sure there's no way she can mistake anything I've said. "I know you're not used to it, but let me help you, and just so we're clear; I don't expect

anything in return for this. When you care about someone, you
want to make their lives easier, not harder."

"Okay," she exhales. "Okay, thank you."

"Text me a picture of his car seat," I remind her. "We'll be
there as soon as we can."

"I'll call the daycare, you'll have to show your ID, and they
may try to charge you since he's staying after closing. Tell them
I'll pay them tomorrow."

"Claudia..." her name is a warning.

"I know, worry about things as they happen, not before."

"Good girl. See you soon."

FINDING the car seat isn't as hard as I imagined it would be,
and installing it isn't either. A quick YouTube video and I've
successfully installed it in my mom's SUV.

You got this - I give myself a little pep talk - as I head to the
daycare. As I get there, I'm sad when I see there's only two cars
parked in the lot. How long ago did they close, and how long
has Jay been sitting in there, waiting on someone to show up
for him.

How many times has he had to do this before?

Steven doesn't deserve this kid or his mother.

Getting out of the SUV, I head to the front door. When I
try it, it's locked. Knocking on the glass, I get the attention of
one of the workers inside.

She walks up to the glass, pointing to the side. It's then I see
the intercom to the side. I press the button. "Hey, I'm here to
pick up Jay Fuller. His mom, Claudia was supposed to call."

"She did," she speaks back into the intercom. "Can you put
your ID up to the glass, please?"

Reaching into my back pocket, I fish out my wallet and grab

my ID. Holding it up, I wait for her to check it, and then step back once she unlocks the door.

"Sorry," she says. "You can never be too careful when you have children in here."

"No, I completely understand, and I'm glad you're careful."

"Dec!" Jay yells as she comes running toward me.

"Hey Jay-Man," I drop to a knee, scooping him up in my arms. "Sorry I'm so late."

"Mama?"

"I'm gonna take you to her," I stand up with him on my hip. "Claud mentioned there might be an extra charge for me being late?"

"Yeah," she glances over at an older woman. "We normally charge five dollars for every ten minutes."

Flipping my phone around so I can see the time. "So sixty bucks, can you run my card? I'd prefer her not to pay for something that's my fault."

"Sure, if you'll come back here," she crooks her finger, signaling for me to follow her.

I do so, putting Jay on the ground, grabbing his hand with mine. Within five minutes, I've paid, we're out, and heading down the road. We're less than two miles away from the daycare when he makes a noise.

"What's wrong, Jay?"' It's then that I smell what's wrong with him. "Oh buddy, do you need a diaper change?"

He nods. I remember some conversation I had with Claudia about how she's trying to potty train him, but it's been hard. Maybe he should've told me, but he didn't, and there's no way I can make him wait until we get to the hospital. Pulling over into the parking lot of a gas station I put the vehicle in park and hurry to get him out, along with the diaper bag.

On the side, there's a men's and women's restroom. Quickly

walking into the men's, I look around for a place to change him and get irritated. There's no changing station.

Walking out, I go toward the women's, and ask someone coming out. "Is there a baby changing station in there?"

"Sure is," she answers, smiling at the two of us.

"Great."

We head in there, and I immediately spot it. Walking over, I get to work. It's been a long time since I changed a diaper, but it's just like riding a bike. Once you do it, you don't forget it.

"What are you doing in here?" A high-pitched voice asks from over my shoulder.

"What does it look like?"

"This is the women's restroom."

"Be that as it may, there isn't a place for me to change him in the men's room, and I refuse to do it on the floor. So go make a complaint if you want, but we'll be out of your hair in five minutes."

She doesn't say anything, and allows me to finish in peace.

CHAPTER 26
CLAUDIA

DECLAN WALKING in with my son on his hip is the hottest thing I've ever seen. Jocelyn is standing beside me, popping her gum. She leans on the counter, whistling under her breath. "If he doesn't look like a Dad I'd like to fuck..."

I sigh. "Right? Although he isn't by blood, he takes better care of him than the real one."

"Who gives a shit. You don't have to be the sperm donor to be a father," she whispers as they walk toward us.

"How's it going?" I ask, reaching out for Jay.

He doesn't want to come to me. Him staying in Declan's arms both kills me and warms my heart. "It's going," Declan gives me a smirk. "I made some lady mad because I used the women's restroom."

My face falls. "You did what?"

"He used the bathroom and needed a diaper change. I pulled over at a gas station, and there was no changing station in the mens restroom. I sure as you know what wasn't going to ask him to lay on the floor while I changed him. I'm a dude, I know how dudes act in bathrooms. So, we went to the women's, where they had a changing station."

"Oh my gosh, that never crossed my mind," I put my hand in front of my mouth. "I mean, ninety-nine percent of the time I'm the one taking him places anyway. I'm so sorry you had to do that."

"No worries, it's a fact of life. It doesn't upset me or anything."

Jocelyn elbows me, clearing her throat loudly at the same time. I sigh, rolling my eyes. "Declan, this is Claudia, Claudia this is Declan."

"Nice to meet you," he gives her a grin.

It's funny to see someone else be as affected by his smile as I am. She's speechless and it's amazing. "Your jaw is hanging on the floor, Joc. Better pick it up."

She frowns over at me, but makes an effort to close her mouth.

"Do you mind if I take a fifteen, so I can get him to the daycare?"

"No," she shakes her head. "Take your time. You hardly ever take a break."

Declan gives her a wave as we turn toward the hallway which will take us to the daycare. "I'm sorry you had a rough time with him. I didn't even think about you not being able to change him if anything happened," I apologize again as we walk through the corridor.

He reaches down, grabbing hold of my hand with his. "I missed you today."

The words are so off-hand, they don't even register at first. But then the butterflies start, and it's as if he's my first everything. "I missed you too," I can't help the grin that spreads across my face. "Thank you for helping, by the way. I didn't expect you to come through, but I'm so glad you did."

"I'm glad I was able to. Mom was more than happy to let me borrow her SUV, and the daycare was nice. They let me know I shouldn't put him in the car seat with his jacket on. Something new I learned today."

"Oh wow, I didn't think about telling you that. Damn, I'm batting a hundred today."

He squeezes my hand. "You've had a day. It's okay. You don't always have to be perfect. If I can help you, I always will. Don't ever be scared to ask for my help, and don't ever assume you're being a burden. I happen to like both of you."

"We like you too."

Together we head down to the daycare. Once we get there, Jay realizes where we're going, jumps out of Declan's arms and runs in to play with his friends. I get him signed in, and then offer to walk Declan out.

"It's still cold, you don't have to walk me the whole way out," he wraps his arm around my neck.

"It's a needed break from work, I remind him."

"True, so I figured I would ask. You got any plans this weekend?"

The way he asks so nonchalantly is the stuff dreams are made of. "No, do you?"

"My only plan is to see if I can get you and Jay-Man to hang out with me."

I cut my eyes over at him. "That could be arranged."

"Text me a grocery list and I'll make sure the two of you have everything you need."

Stopping in the middle of the hallway, I look around to make sure we're relatively alone, before I throw myself into his arms and give him the biggest kiss. "I don't know what I did to deserve you, but it's going to take a hell of a lot for me to let you go."

CHAPTER 27

DECLAN

"HEARD YOU PLAYED DADDY TODAY," Riley quips as I have a seat at the dinner table. A few times a month we try to have dinner as a family.

"Oh yeah, who'd you hear that from?" I take a bite of the garlic bread on the table.

"Jocelyn."

"Wait, you're friends with her too? Is there anything you and Claudia don't share?"

She wrinkles her nose. "You. She hasn't shared a damn thing about what the two of you have been doing, and for that shit I am thankful."

"Me and you both." I fling back at her. "I don't want you to know about my life, and I sure don't want to know about yours."

"What do you mean he played Daddy?" Mom asks as she brings a steaming pan of shrimp scampi to the table while Dad follows with a large bowl of salad.

Oh here we go. "Claudia needed someone to help her, and I did. It's not that big of a deal."

We all take a seat, and start fixing our plates, when Mom looks at me. It's the serious kind of stare I haven't gotten since I was a teenager. "It is a big deal, Dec. There aren't many people she can count on, and the fact she knows she can count on you? That means everything to her."

"How come you never told me you were a single mom?" I ask, taking another bite of my garlic bread. "Don't you think that would've been something good to share with me?"

The rest of the table looks uncomfortable as I pin them with my gaze. Dad clears his throat. "I'm going to say this to you once, and I don't want to hear about it again. When I adopted Riley, I made the decision that we were a family. We'd never have to mention it again because it was painful for your mom and sister. You don't know what they went through, and their trauma isn't yours Dec. You were blessed to be brought up in a family who loved you and has never judged you for the decisions you've made. You wanna blame somebody? Blame me. You have questions? Ask me. I'm not trying to be a dick, but that wasn't a good time in any of our lives. The end justified the means, but it was hard getting there."

The younger me may have questioned his reasons, may have wanted a better answer, but the more I hang out with Claudia and Jay, the more I'm realizing things aren't black and white. That multiple things can be true at the same time, and just maybe I'm not privy to all of them.

"I understand, and if either of you ever wanna talk about your experiences, I'm here to listen. I'm sorry if I came across as not being sensitive to what you've dealt with. No one told me about what happened before, and now that I know better, I can do better. I'm sorry."

Mom gets up from her seat and comes around the table, holding her arms out for me. Gratefully I collapse into them, wrapping mine around her. "I know as far as you're concerned,

I never kept anything from you, so this had to be a surprise. You had to feel as if you weren't part of a family secret and that had to be painful. We've all made mistakes. The important thing is we learn from them, and from each other. So tell us, is there something we can do in order to help you with Claudia?"

Sitting down, I shovel a forkful of food into my mouth. I take my time chewing, trying to get my thoughts together, then swallow. "Tell me that I'm not trying to push her? I want to be in her life, I want her to call me when she needs help. At the same time, I want her to feel as if she's strong enough to do things on her own."

Dad speaks. "It's a hard balance, but all you have to do is be consistent. You don't have to know all the answers, or do the right thing all the time, but just being there means more than you know."

Riley takes a drink from her glass, before putting it down. She's the one person I've wanted to hear from, and she's also the one keeping her mouth shut. Until she doesn't. "Claudia plays a role she thinks people expect from her. It's hard for her to allow people to see the real her. If she's being vulnerable then she trusts you. If she's showing that things aren't always perfect, you're getting the real her. Keep doing what you're doing. It's all the right things, I promise."

"Thank you, and I hope you're okay with us being together. I haven't asked you, and I should've."

Riley shrugs. "The only thing I want is for both of you to be happy. I'm warning you though, I know you both. It's not going to be easy, especially with how stubborn the both of you are. Promise me if she tries to push you away, you won't give up on her."

Although I can never imagine her doing it, I nod. "I promise, and I hope I never have to put this one into reality."

"Here, here," Dad raises his glass.

We all do the same, but I have a feeling this is one woman I'll be fighting for.

CHAPTER 28
CLAUDIA

"ARE you ready to spend the weekend with Declan?" I ask Jay, packing his bag and mine. I've switched shifts and called in as many favors as I can to get today and tomorrow off.

"Yes," he yells, clapping his hands. "Riley too?"

"Riley will be there, I confirm."

I'm getting the last of the stuff together when Mom walks in the room. "You're going to be gone today and tomorrow right. Are you going to spend the night there?"

"I already told you I'm going to. Do you have something you want to say to me?"

"Look, you've already had one accidental pregnancy. You don't need two," she says it so matter of factly I'd like to wipe the smug sneer off her face.

"You can rest assured things are taken care of. When I got pregnant with Jay, I wasn't on birth control. I have been since I gave birth to him. You don't need to worry about me."

"Obviously I should've worried about you more a couple years ago."

This conversation is pissing me off. "Mom, we'll be back on Monday. Have a great weekend."

She doesn't even say bye to Jay as we leave. Somehow I have to figure out a way to get us out of the situation we're in. It's a never-ending chain of events that lead in disappointment except for anything having to do with the Tennyson family.

Declan is waiting outside when we get there, ready to help me carry everything in. "Did you have any trouble?" He asks, reaching out his hand to take the diaper bag and overnight bag from me.

"No, Mom was happy to see us go. I think as happy as we are to be here."

He reaches down, kissing me on the cheek and tousling Jay's hair. "Well my mom has been cooking up a storm for y'all. She can't wait for Jay to try her chocolate chip cookies."

"She shouldn't have. I feel bad she went to the trouble."

"Trust me, she wanted to. She's had fun." He leads me up the stairway to his parents apartment. "Let her get it over with," he laughs. "We're here," he announces as we walk in.

"Welcome, welcome," Mom greets them. "Jay, I made cookies, do you like cookies?"

"He loves cookies," I answer for him.

"So do I," Riley interrupts as she blows in like the force of nature she is.

"Riley," he exclaims, dropping down from my arms and rushing toward her.

"Look," Riley whispers as she comes over to us. "I'm not saying I haven't noticed the way you've been smiling from ear to ear, how you're more relaxed that you've been in a long time, or how happy my brother makes you. I've also been noticing that you haven't answered my texts or offered to hang out with me, but I'm going to tell you, I understand it."

"Riley, I'm sorry," I reach over, wrapping my arms around her.

"It's okay, when ya fall in love, that guy takes up all your time. Trust me, I get it. Remember Frankie?"

I giggle loudly, rolling my eyes. "Who could forget Frankie?"

She raises her hand. "Girl, I do every time I think about how stupid I was. But I get it. When the new wears off, I'll be here and we'll still be best friends."

"I love you, Riles."

"Love you, too. Now let me get this boy some cookies, and then him and Aunt Riley can go watch some movies, while you and Declan have a nice afternoon."

WE'VE BEEN TALKING all afternoon and night. Where our first couple of nights together were characterized by stolen kisses and sexual activities, this day and night has been nothing but family time and confessing secrets.

"What was your biggest regret?" He asks, taking a drink from his glass of bourbon.

"Not Jay, but Steven. When I was a kid all I wanted was to be a mom. So I could give a child the type of mom I always wanted. Mine has never been the kind to celebrate the small wins, or even be there for the big mistakes. I mean, don't get me wrong, when I found out I was pregnant with Jay, she was there. Not in the way I wanted her to be, but she was there. When Steven told me he wanted me to get an abortion, and I told him no, she stood by my side."

"She should've, Claud. She's your mom."

Not wanting to talk about her, I change the subject. "Do you know Jay's never stayed overnight with Steven?"

"Are you kidding me? He's never had his son for an overnight?" His voice is as surprised as I imagined it would be.

"Never. He's supposed to with our custody agreement, but every time he's supposed to have him, he makes an excuse. Too busy, or he just flakes. Half the time he doesn't even call. I just have to assume he's not going to show up. If he ever does, I'll be surprised."

He takes another drink. "One thing I can promise you, Claud. I'll always show up."

"Trust me, Dec. I don't doubt that for a minute."

CHAPTER 29
CLAUDIA

RAIN IS POURING onto the remnants of the last snow storm we had, making rivers of muddy goo as I make my way out of my last class. All I want is to go home and hang out with my son, maybe called Declan and see what he's doing, but instead, I have to go to work.

As I get closer to my car, I see someone standing next to the driver's side door. Gripping my purse tighter to me, I feel for the pepper spray.

When I see it's Steven, I breathe a sigh of relief and drop it. "What do you want?" I shout over the rain.

"I heard you let some other man take care of my son earlier this week."

"What exactly was I supposed to do? It was your day to pick him up and bring him to me. That's all I asked of you, Steven, but you couldn't even do that. I was stuck at work. One of us has to pay for him. It sure as hell isn't you, considering how far behind on child support you are. Hardly anyone will do me a favor anymore, because I've asked so many times, and it's because of you," I poke at his chest.

"Don't touch me," he reaches out, grabbing my finger. "It's because of you that you've run out of people to ask. You just use people until they're sick of you. Like you used me to get the child you wanted so badly. You didn't give a shit about my thoughts and feelings. I begged you to get an abortion because I knew I'd be a shitty father. Here you are, though, bitching because I won't help you."

He couldn't have slapped me harder than these words hit me. "And here you are, bitching because some other man stepped into your place and acted like a father to the child you ignore most of the time. It shouldn't matter to you, Steven. In fact, you should be thanking him. He's taking care of shit you've never thought to take care of."

Steven gives me a smile that doesn't go to his eyes. It's beyond scary, the

way his eyes get this blank look. "It does matter to me. Not because of Jay. Because of you. You've made my life a living hell, Claudia. There's a warrant attached to my name for child support, meaning I can't get an above-board job, ever. There's this kid who runs around calling me Dad, and that's for life. I'm going to have to be the person he blames for his shitty child-hood the rest of his life."

"And you could change that," I argue. "Sign away your parental rights, or be an actual father. There are ways out of this."

"No, I don't want to give you the benefit of it. You shouldn't have lied to me

about being on birth control."

"I didn't lie to you. I told you I'd been on antibiotics and it might not be as effective and you should wear a condom. You said it wouldn't feel as good and refused. We were both to blame, Steven. The last thing I want, is for Jay to have to pay for our mistakes," I press against him, trying to get some space in between the two of us.

"That would make you happy, wouldn't it?"

"It would make my life. If I could just get rid of you."

He steps closer, leaning in so that he's inches away from my face. "Which

means I refuse to give you the benefit of it. You keep fucking around, Claudia, I'll sue you for custody of our son. You know I don't have money, but my family does, and if I grease the wheels of my grandmother, and finally tell her she has a great-grandchild, no expense will be spared. She'll go into debt to get what she wants, and she'll take you down. You know she'll find out every secret you're hiding and broadcast it to anyone who cares to listen. The little business your boyfriend's family has? It'll be gone too. You think you're worth all of that, Claudia?"

He hits me where he knows it hurts. I will never think that much of myself. Self-confidence and assurance are where I fail every time. "It's over, okay. Just don't threaten Jay."

He smirks. "You're easy. In more ways than one."

As I get in my car, the tears fall, and I'm trying to figure out how I'm going

to live the rest of my life wondering what might have been.

CHAPTER 30
DECLAN

MY PHONE BUZZES with the sound of an incoming text. When I see Claudia's smiling face, my heart pounds a little faster.

> C: I know this is coming out of nowhere for you, but I have to protect my son. We can't see each other anymore. No matter how badly I want this, Dec. It's not going to work. Thank you for the best couple of months I've had.

> D: What the fuck, Claud?

> C: I wish I could explain to you everything going through my head right now, but I can't. Thank you for giving me something to smile about. I'm sorry we couldn't make this work, but he's threatened my life with Jay.

> D: Let me help you.

> C: I don't need you to always figure out my problems for me, Dec.

> D: I don't want to figure them out for you, I want you to let me be a part of the solution.

> C: I'm sorry, but I can't. Jay is the most important person in my life and I refuse to make him feel as if he comes in second to anyone.

My stomach aches as I realize what she's saying. She's convinced herself that in order for her to have a life, she's the one who's going to have to make the sacrifices. There's only one thing I can think of to make her stay.

> D: I love you.

> C: I love you too, but sometimes love isn't enough, Declan. I'll always remember you, and the fire escape, and a glass of bourbon.

With a growl, I throw my phone at the wall, sliding down to the floor.

"Declan? What's wrong?" Riley's voice is full of concern as she comes into my apartment. Usually I'd be annoyed at her for coming in without knocking, but right now I'm thankful.

"Claudia," I take in a few deep breaths, trying not to hyperventilate.

"What's wrong with her? Is Jay okay?"

"She said we can't see each other anymore. That Steven threatened her and Jay."

"Declan," she rushes over, holding her arms open. "I am so sorry."

I can't get myself up off the floor, so she slides down to where I am, holding me tightly against her. "I can't blame her," I cry for the first time since I was a kid. "She loves her son, and everything she does is for him, but was I so easy to let go of?"

"I can promise you it wasn't easy for her," she whispers. "You and I both know she doesn't give herself much grace, and she never thinks of herself first. She was with you, her happiness was something she wasn't willing to put on the backburner, not anymore. Whatever happened with the two of them, it must've been bad."

It can't be as bad as I'm feeling right now. I had allowed myself to start planning a life with her, one that included her and Jay. I was even beginning to imagine more kids we could add to the mix, a ring on her finger, and giving her my last name. "I just wish she would trust me enough to let me help her with whatever it is."

"You and I both know she likes to handle things on her own."

"I do, and so do I. While I appreciate you being here, I need some time alone."

"Dec, I don't think it'd be a good idea to leave you on your own right now."

"Go Riley, I'm not good company."

She looks like she wants to argue, but luckily she doesn't. Somehow I manage to pick myself up off the floor, and drag my body over to the island. Grabbing the bottle of bourbon we shared, I pour a glass, drink it down, and hope it'll wash all my sorrows away.

CHAPTER 31

CLAUDIA

> C: Steven I need your help. If you're not going to let me have someone in my life who was a fucking partner to me, you have to step up.

STILL THERE'S no answer to the texts I've sent to him. Out of sheer desperation, I send one over to Riley.

> C: I hate to do this, but I need help. Can you watch Jay this afternoon?

> R: I can't believe you'd ask me that after what you did to my brother. You're my best friend, but I need time to get over what you did to Declan. He's devastated, and I don't know how I feel about you right now, either.

That breaks my heart, knowing that I've hurt him as much as I'm hurting right now. If I could change any of this, I would, but life doesn't always work out how we want it to. I'm reminding myself of this every day as I'm trying to make it.

Tears fall out of my eyes, making rivers down my cheeks.

Out of desperation, I make one more phone call.

Declan

"I HOPE you have some food because I am fucking starving," I announce my arrival at my parents. I've been trying to get back on a strict schedule since Claudia broke up with me. The last week has been a rollercoaster, but the two nights in a row, I've come to my parents to have food, better than drinking my dinner, anyway.

"Dec!" That voice is enough to melt the stone that's become my heart over the past week.

"Jay man, what are you doing here?"

Mom looks at me over his head. "Claudia needed someone to watch him, and I offered."

"I guess S can make demands and not see them through, huh?" I whisper-hiss back at her over his head.

"She's in a tough spot, Declan."

While I can appreciate it, I'm still fucking pissed over how we left things, but I refuse to punish Jay for it. I hold him tightly to me. "We're all in a tough spot. Including my heart."

"Declan, I need you to realize something. Not every decision she makes will be because she wants to screw you over, or because it's an easy one to make. Most of the time when you're putting your children first, there are sacrifices that have to be made, and you have to disappoint someone to make them. You're an adult, and I promise if you're patient with her, she will come back to you."

"Mom, normally I'd believe you, but right now I can't find it in myself to do so," I admit, sighing. "This feels like the end of a great relationship, instead of the beginning of something perfect."

She gives me a glare. "This isn't about you, Declan. It's about her, and it's about this little boy. When you realize that, she'll come back to you."

I wish I could believe her, especially with Jay on my hip, but it all seems so hopeless.

"I'll believe it when I see it."

CHAPTER 32
CLAUDIA

"THANK YOU FOR WATCHING HIM," I brush Jay's hair out of his sleeping face.

"It's really no problem," Hadley folds her arms over her chest. "I miss having babies around here, but I really think you should go talk to my son while you have a few minutes. He'd like to hear from you, and as someone who was in your shoes a lifetime ago, you're going to wish you'd done it."

Against my better judgment I know she's right, I already miss him, already wish I would've done things in a much different way than I did. "I shouldn't have texted him. I should've at least had the guts to give him a goodbye in person."

She nods, but her voice is understanding when she speaks. "We do the best we can with what we have. Sometimes that's a text message, sometimes it's seeing someone in person. I'm not here to judge you. I've been in your shoes before, but I also care about my son. I think he would do with a little more closure than what he's had."

"I'll be back in a bit."

"He's asleep, and he'll stay that way," Hadley assures me.

The walk to Declan's apartment feels much longer than it normally does. When I get there, I knock on the door and wait for him to answer it. He does, holding a glass of bourbon. "What are you doing here?"

I shrug. "I needed to see you."

"I wanted to see you days ago, but you refused to do that, why should I see you now?"

Taking this one moment of my life in my hands, I grab hold of his shoulders, push him inside, and plant the kiss I've always wanted to give him on the lips. He makes a noise of surprise in the back of his throat, and his arms go around me, cupping my ass, and pulling my legs around his waist.

Declan

I CAN'T HELP but feel this is a goodbye as I thrust inside her. Our foreheads are pressed together, and we're breathing each other's breaths.

"I wish we could stay together," she whispers. "If I could make it work, I would. I love you, Dec."

My eyes close as I relish the words from her lips, wishing I could take them and hold onto them forever. If wishes were gifts, I'd both open and give this one every day.

"I love you, too," I whisper back at her, rolling my hips in and out, trying to reach her heart. If I could force her to stay with the power of my love, I would.

This joining is both slow and fast. It'll never last long enough, and it'll be over before I know it. The climax washes over me in waves, almost in stages. The way she clasps around me, the same thing happens for her.

As we break apart, and clean up, we're quiet.

"I have to go get Jay. It's past time for him to be in bed," she speaks softly, almost as if she's scared to disrupt the spell that's been weaved around us.

"You can stay here," I offer.

"No I can't," she shakes her head. "If you could've seen Steven. It was almost as if he was another person when he was threatening me. What few people know about him, is he's a member of the Waldorf family."

"Are you fucking kidding me?" They own at least three-fourths of the block we're on right now, along with another three-fourths of the city. The money they have is not insignificant, and neither is the clout.

"No, they hardly ever claim him because he's a black sheep, the screw up. Everyone else is either a doctor or a lawyer, and he was lucky to graduate high school. For a while I felt sorry for him, wanted him to realize he didn't have to be perfect for someone to love him. I thought I could be the person who saved him," she laughs now. "Instead he's the person who gave me the greatest gift and then hurt me in ways no other person has ever attempted to."

"This isn't about him, though," I remind her. "This is about us. If you're willing to let him control your life like this, then he's always going to do so. Don't you think it's time to show him you can stand on your own two feet? That he has nothing to say about how you live the rest of your life?"

She wipes at the corner of her eyes. "I don't think I'm that strong yet, Dec. So I have to say goodbye."

"No," I reach out and grab her. "This is goodbye for now, not goodbye forever."

CHAPTER 33

CLAUDIA

ALTHOUGH THE DAYS are getting longer and there's more sunshine than snow, I'm in a deep hole I'm unsure I'll ever be able to escape from.

I'd been seeing colors.

Smiling.

Hoping.

Making plans for the future.

Then it was all ripped out of my hands. Happiness like I'd never had made the day brighter, and then it was all gone. Like a magic trick, right there for me to grab, and then as I made the lunge - poof - like a cloud of dust.

Steven is a bastard.

I now know he's going to make the rest of my life while we're co-parenting a living hell.

"Claudia, did you hear what I said?"

Glancing up at my professor, I shake my head. "I'm sorry, I didn't."

"Why don't you stay after class then, I have a few things I'd like to talk to you about."

Shit.

I know I'm screwing up, and this is the worst time for me to do so. I have three classes until I get my degree, and this is one of them. "Yes ma'am."

The rest of the class passes in a blur as I wonder what she's going to say. If there's one thing I never want to do, it's disappoint people in places of authority. A holdover from when I had to admit to my mom I was pregnant and I'd be continuing to live under her roof longer than I'd anticipated. As students start getting up and making their way to the exit, I keep my seat.

I've never been one for confrontation, and as I've been having to deal with Steven more, it's giving me anxiety I've never had previously. She gazes at me as the class empties.

Finally, I work up the nerve to get up from my chair and make my way to the front. "Professor Wilkes," I nod, gripping my hands into fists.

"Have a seat," she offers.

Because my knees are knocking, I gratefully take the seat she's offering. "What did you want to talk about?"

"Let's not beat around the bush here, we're both adults and we're both parents. I don't want to tell you what to do, and I'd never pretend to know your life, but let me tell you a few things I do know. You're incredibly smart, you're one of the most intelligent students I've ever had, and you're dedicated to your child. I also know you're a single mother who has had to sacrifice an amazing amount to be in this class and to get as far as you have. What I don't understand is why you're willing to screw it all up here at the last minute."

I hang my head, because I don't know what to say. I sigh heavily, feeling as if the weight of the world is on my shoulders. "I have worked hard for this. Worked, so fucking hard. I've been a single mother from the jump, and I finally opened myself up to another man," my bottom lip quivers, and I allow the tears to come. "But the father of my son found out, and he's made my life a living hell since. He's told me I'm not allowed to see the guy, and he's threatened me. It's thrown me into this depression I'm scared I'm not going to be able to get out of," I whisper. "I've lost the man I love, and two best friends. My son has lost someone he cares about more than he cares about his father. We spent the best weekend with him, and now it's going to be some memory no other guy he calls Dad will live up to."

"What do you mean by two?" She questions, leaning forward and placing a hand on mine.

"His sister is my childhood best friend and he somehow became another one in the short amount of time we were together. I'm walking around with these clouds of gloom over me. I want to be as happy as I was a week ago, but I can't concentrate on anything," I explain.

"This is what I'm going to tell you," Professor Wilkes inhales deeply. "Life is never going to be perfect. We can plan it to our hearts desire, and there will always be something that messes us up. I was a single mother, too. With all the plans in the world."

"How did those plans work out?" I ask quietly.

"I'm here, aren't I? It took me a lot longer than I imagined, but this was my dream. Just because I had to do things slower and they took longer, didn't mean they didn't happen. So don't sabotage yourself, Claudia. You're a smart woman, who has a bright future. Don't let one wrinkle in your plans derail the whole thing. Do you understand what I'm saying?"

It hits me like a ton of bricks. I've spent so much time thinking about where I should be, and what I would change if I could, that I haven't appreciated what I have in front of me. "I do. I'll make this work. I'm sorry."

"No need to apologize to me. Just do better for yourself.

You deserve it, Claudia."

For the first time in a long while, I believe it.

CHAPTER 34
DECLAN

"SON OF A BITCH," the words work their way from between my gritted teeth as blood pours from my hand.

"Oh Dec, you need to get that looked at," Dad winces. He reaches over, grabbing a clean towel to staunch the flow. "Let me drive you, c'mon."

"Claudia's working," I groan.

"What's going on between the two of you?" He questions. "You haven't talked about her, and your mom watched Jay the other day. I didn't ask because she didn't look like she wanted to talk about it, and if there's anything I've learned, it's not to ask your mom shit she doesn't want to talk about."

I'm holding onto my hand as Dad helps me in the passenger side of his truck. Nausea rolls through my stomach as I get a glimpse at the blood through the bandage we've fixed. Closing my eyes, I start to tell him about Claudia.

"Jay's dad is a member of the Waldorf family," I hiss.

"Fucking what?" Dad questions, looking over at me. "Why is she struggling so bad?"

"He's not the favorite of the family, but I guess if he pressures them, then they'll do what he wants, and right now he wants to make her life miserable."

Dad hisses. *What a fucker.*

"Exactly."

"Reminds me of Riley's biological dad. He did the same type of shit to Hadley. You see how it's worked out for them. I have a feeling it's going to work out for you too. Even if it doesn't seem like it right now."

"How do you know that?" I need desperately for my Dad to make me believe in all the best that life has to offer. As a kid he was always that person for me.

"Because she loves you, and you love her. That's the type of stuff that can't be imagined or denied for long. He can try to fuck you all over, he can try to make money talk. It'll work for a while, but it won't work forever. You have to believe in each other."

Normally I'm willing to blindly follow him with whatever he has to say. This is the man who has guided me my entire life, and he's never steered me wrong, but right now I don't know that he's understanding how this life goes for some people. "I don't know, I'm just not willing to accept this blindly like I do everything else you say. There's so much more at stake here than anything else."

"No, I get it. It was the same with Riles and Hadley, but this was the thing. I couldn't give up on them. Once I gave up, what else did they have? A father and an ex-husband who didn't give a shit about them. I know me," he points at his chest. "I know what I'm willing to do for those two ladies, and I knew he was never going to live up to what I was willing to do. I know patience isn't your strong suit, but it's what you have to have."

We get to the hospital, and he drops me off at the ER.

"You don't have to stay if you don't want to. I'll call you when I'm ready for you to come and get me."

"Are you sure? You're an adult and I wanna respect your wishes," he continues.

"I'm sure. I'm probably gonna need a tetanus shot and some stitches."

He gives me a wave, and I head into the entrance.

It takes a few minutes, but I'm put on the list and sent to triage. There aren't many people waiting, so they immediately send me back to a room. Before they can register me, a nurse comes in.

"I heard you got a heck of a cut, and could probably use some pain medication," she says, holding a bag of medicine. "Along with some antibiotics," she whistles as she sees the grease on my fingers.

"I'm a mechanic."

"I can see. Let's get an IV started, I'll get some antibiotics and some pain medication going, and then we'll get a doctor in here. Sound good?"

"Sounds good to me."

There's a knock at the door, and in walks Claudia. "Hey, I'm here to register you."

When she looks up, she notices I'm sitting there. "Declan, oh my God, are you okay?"

"Had an accident at the shop. Luckily I didn't accidentally almost cut something off, but I do have a deep cut."

I wish we were alone, but I'll take what I can get when it comes to Claudia Wilson.

CHAPTER 35
CLAUDIA

TRUE TO FORM, Steven is thirty minutes late.

And I'm still shaken from seeing Declan at the hospital with a blood soaked bandage wrapped around his hand a week ago. I've been doing nothing but thinking about it. All I can imagine is, what if he'd done something a lot worse? What if he'd been lying in that hospital bed and I wasn't one of the people who was called and notified? That hurts more than I care to admit.

Shoving my head back against the wall, I sigh roughly.

"Mom, I'm hungry," Jay whines.

I hadn't fed him because I assumed Steven would take care of it.

"I know, we're gonna wait a few more minutes for your Dad to get here, and then I'll take you to get something to eat, okay?"

I look at my phone. There's no message from Steven. *C'mon, don't do this to him again.*

"Declan," Jay yells at the man himself walking toward us.

"Hey," he greets Jay, before nodding at me.

"How are you doing?" I ask. "I wanted to text you to see

how you're holding up, but figured it might be hard for you to text with your hand like that."

"Yeah, it's been a pain in the ass. I've been doing orders and answering phone calls, making appointments. I'm not the best customer service person, but it's what I can do right now," he shrugs.

"When do you get the stitches out?"

"I'm seeing the doctor today," he nods toward one of the offices in the building. "I'll be able to figure out when that is."

It's awkward being so close to him and knowing I don't have the right to touch him the way I did a few weeks ago. I wish things were different and they hadn't ended the way they did between us.

"I wish the same," he says.

"I didn't mean to say that out loud," I push my hair behind my ears, trying to hide the embarrassment.

"I bet you didn't. What are the two of you doing standing outside, anyway?"

"I'm hungry," Jay announces.

"I'm sorry," he answers, looking down at him. "When was the last time you ate?"

"This afternoon," he sighs. "So long ago."

"What are you all doing here?" Declan asks again.

"They're waiting on me."

My head whips around, looking at Steven. His eyes are bright, pupils are pinpoints. I've had suspicions for a long time, but I've never had the evidence to call him on it. "Where were you?" I ask, trying to buy us a few minutes.

"None of your damn business. Give me his diaper bag, and we'll be on our way."

"No," I shake my head. "There's no way he's going with you."

"How do you think you're gonna stop me? He's my son.

You can't keep me from seeing him." He argues, reaching forward to grab Jay's hand.

I step in between them. "No, you're not taking him. I'll call the police and they'll arrest you. I bet you have it on you too. Grandma's money will only take you so far, Steven. You really need to get your shit together, or you won't be seeing him again. Now that I have proof of what you're doing, I'll spend every cent and every spare second I have making sure you don't hurt him."

"You bitch," he snarls, taking a step closer to me. "You can't do this.

"I can, and I will."

CHAPTER 36
DECLAN

MY HAND ACHES, not because the stitches in it are painful, although they are, but because I want to jack this motherfucker's jaw more than I've ever wanted anything.

"I think she said he's not going with you, and if I were you I'd listen to what she said. I'd also not call her a bitch again unless you want me to break my fist on your nose."

He steps up to me, but I'm taller. His forehead rests at my nose. "No one asked you what you think, and you have no skin in this game. He's not your son, she isn't your girl."

There's a red haze where my vision should be. I've never had it be so clear, the fact I want to kick another person's ass. I step up to him so that we're nose to nose. "Let me ask you something, has your son ever stayed overnight with you? Have you ever helped Claudia when she's requested it? Have you ever paid a cent of child support? Funny how you're claiming that this was your girl and he's your son, yet you've never done any of these things, and I've done them all."

"You think that makes you a better man than me?" Steven

tilts his head back so he can look me in the eye. "She's a pity fuck for you, isn't she?"

Claudia gasps, and the hand with the stitches connects with his face in a satisfying crack. He falls to the concrete, hand over his eye. "No, she's not. Just like I don't take pity on your son either. Both of them deserve to have someone who loves them and will take care of them without making them feel as if they're unloved. You don't understand how lucky you are, piece of shit."

"Lucky?" He laughs. "I have her bitching to me every day about how I don't spend time with my son. About how I owe her money, and that I'm never going to be good enough. I thought I could get her to kill him," he shoves his finger in the direction of Jay.

Jay starts crying. "Get him and take him to the car," I direct Claudia. "Neither one of you need to hear this."

I watch as she picks him up and runs to her car.

Now that they're both out of earshot, I step up to the fucker. "Here's what you're going to do. When she asks you, you're going to sign over parental rights, and you're going to let her go. You don't want her, you don't want him, all you're doing is making shit difficult."

"What makes you think I'll give her the satisfaction?" He spits blood to the side.

"Oh I think you will," I give him a grin. "There's a few things you don't know about me. My dad was in prison, and he's done bad things."

Truth is, I have no idea what he did, all I know is he was in prison.

"He loves Claudia and Jay. He's willing to do whatever it takes to make them happy. Which means he would do whatever she asks him to when it comes to you. Don't believe me? Ask around. The only other people who own property on my block besides your family, is mine. I'm not scared of you, and neither is he."

The high must be wearing off, because his pupils are starting to become normal. "What's in it for me?"

"You won't owe child support anymore. I'll take care of them, and I'll have something written that legally absolves you. Again, when we ask for parental rights to be terminated; which will be when we get married, you sign off and don't give us any shit. If you do, I'll make your life a living hell. We do work for a lot of MC's, Steven, and a couple of them are one percenter's. They'll do anything I ask. You getting a picture of what I'm saying?"

He swallows roughly. Everyone knows we do a lot of work, and they know we work for some people who only care about their bikes. They wear patches, cuts, and colors.

"Crystal clear picture."

"Good, now go."

Steven looks as if he wants to say something else, but he doesn't. Instead he makes for his shitty little compact car, gets in, and squeals tires out of the parking lot.

CHAPTER 37
CLAUDIA

"THESE WERE DELIVERED FOR YOU," Jocelyn says as she points to the flowers at the nurses station.

"For me?"

"Well they sure as hell weren't delivered for me," she laughs.

I reach over, grabbing the card from the holder.

Claudia,

I understand, more than I ever have, what it means to love someone. Flaws and all. I have them, you have them, and together I want us to live a perfectly imperfect life.

I love you, I love Jay, and that's never going to change.

I'll wait as long as I have to, but just in

case I don't have to wait. Look up, I'll be waiting for you.

Love,
Declan

LOOKING UP, Declan is standing a few feet down the hallway, Jay on his hip. It's become one of my favorite pictures. So that I have it with me at all times, I pull my cell phone out and take one. The smile on my face will never be able to be wiped off as I walk faster to meet them halfway.

"You got my flowers?" He smirks.

"I did, and I know this isn't going to be easy. We have a lot of stuff in our way. I still have to finish school, I'll transfer jobs, and I need to get out of my mom's apartment, but what I can promise you is I'll let you help me. I know I've made it difficult in the past, but the way you stood up for me with Steven? No one has ever done that before. I realize for us to be a couple it has to be a partnership, and I've wanted to stand on my own for so long, I forgot what that even meant. I can learn, though. You're a great teacher," I smirk right back at him.

"Damn right I am," he laughs. "I have some promises to make to you too. When shit gets tough, I'm not going to make you handle it by yourself. I'm going to remind you what it is to depend on your partner, and I'm going to show you exactly what that means. I promise to treat Jay like my own, to do whatever he needs to feel comfortable with me, and us together. My family will love him, and together we'll build the life we've both always dreamed of," he holds out his hand. "Come on this journey with me?"

I clasp my hand with his. "There's absolutely no one else I'd rather be on a journey with."

"Thank God," he whispers, pulling me in and planting a kiss on me that rivals any of the best movies.

In the background, I hear Jocelyn shouting and clapping.

And for the first time in my life, I know what it means to be the star of my own love story.

EPILOGUE

Declan

FOUR YEARS Later

"RUN JAY, RUN!" Claudia's voice is the loudest up in the stands as our son makes his way around the bases. Because I'm the coach I'm screaming too, but she's got me beat.

"C'mon Jay-Man," Dad's voice is now competing.

Waving my arm, I'm trying to get him to home plate by force of will. If I could run those bases for him, I would. He's fast, but he's got to pick it up if he's going to beat the throw coming from the outfield. The other team (swear to God) has a twelve-year-old playing on the six to ten squad.

It's going to be close as he rounds third. "Kick it into high gear buddy, c'mon!"

He does just that, dirt kicking up behind him from his

cleats as he digs in and makes every step count. That's something we've been working on in practice the past few months. His arms are pumping, propelling him forward, and the name *Tennyson* sprawled across his back makes my breath catch each time I see it.

As he gets to home plate, the throw comes in.

"Slide!" I scream, my throat aching from the beating it's taking.

He hears and performs a perfect head-first slide, the gloved-covered tips of his fingers touching the base at the same time the catcher swipes at him. I'd hate to be this damn referee.

We all watch with bated breath as we wait for the declaration.

"Safe!"

The crowd and all of us erupt in cheers and hollering. This means we're going to the championship game.

"Dad," he yells, running toward me.

It still makes my heart stutter when he calls me that. I made it very clear when Claudia and I decided to make a go of this that I wouldn't expect him to call me anything other than Dec. It'd taken him a few months, and the moment he'd called me Dad, I'd had to make sure he was talking to me. Then I'd had to go to the bathroom and cry.

Tears of gratitude and love.

This kid has had it from the first moment I met him. I catch him when runs up to me, picking him up off the ground and spinning him around. It's harder than it used to be. He's gotten bigger, and he's growing up quicker than I like.

Leaning down, I move his hat out of the way, hugging him tightly. "I'm proud of you, Jay-Man." Two years into our marriage and I'd gotten Steven to give up his parental rights so I could adopt him.

"Thanks Dad, if it hadn't been for us practicing the slide, I wouldn't have made it."

"You would've. You're a smart kid, you would've figured it out."

"Jay!" The voice of my wife causes us to turn around.

Pride and love squeeze my heart as I see her walking toward us. Riley's on one side, my mom on her other. She's nine months pregnant - due today actually - and glowing. I'd tried to get her to stay at home since the sun is out and it's hot, but she'd refused, whether they won or lost; she wanted to be here.

"Mom, you should be careful," he runs over to her, patting her stomach.

"You shouldn't tell me what to do," she rolls her eyes. "You did amazing out there, and I'm so proud of you." She leans in, kissing him on the cheek.

"Thank you, do you mind if I go to my friends?"

"No, go have fun."

I watch as he runs off, jumping into the circle of his friends.

"I'm proud of you too," she walks over to me, wrapping her arms around my waist. "You did good, Coach."

"These kids make me look good," I joke.

"Nope, that's the pants they have you wear," she jokes back. "But for real, I do have something I need to talk to you about."

"What's that, sweet girl?"

"I've been in labor the last two innings."

I'm sure my eyes bug out of my head. "Fucking what? Why didn't you tell someone?"

"Because I've done this before. I'm telling you we have time."

"Well I haven't done this before, " I argue. "And I say let's get to the hospital."

"Let's not make a big deal out of it, just in case it's false labor," she whispers.

Fuck that.

"We're heading to the hospital. Claudia's in labor." I announce as I usher her toward the parking lot. "Dad," I point to my parents. "Y'all got Jay-Man?"

"Of course."

My sister runs toward us. "If you need anything let me know, and I might not have mentioned it lately, but I love you two and the family you've made."

"Love you too, I'll let you know ASAP."

Claudia has her head turned trying to talk as I pull her to the brand new SUV we just bought in preparation for this. When I help her into the passenger seat, she puts her hands on my shoulders. "I love you, Dec. You're already the best Dad in the world, and you've been the best husband I could ever have imagined. This is just another step in our lives together. No need to be nervous."

"Where you're concerned. I'll always be nervous," I cup her cheek in my palm. "I love you."

"Love you too, and at the end of the day? That's all I need to know."

My heart jumping in my chest, I head over to the driver's side, ready to expand our family and start the rest of our lives.

The End

SHADOWS
ISABELLA

"YOU WANT ME TO WHAT?" The words stumble out of my mouth and I raise my eyebrow, hoping to convey just how confused I am at what he just said.

He takes off his glasses, rubbing his eyes vigorously with the tips of his fingers. I let him sit with what I've asked, not wanting to frustrate him any more than I already have. Hopefully, giving him a few moments without my voice will lead him to re-think what he's requesting of me.

"Isabella, you have to prove how much you want this."

My stomach drops as his gravelly declaration sinks in. He hasn't reconsidered; he's doubling down. "What does me interviewing Shadows Sampson have to do with any of this?"

"Shadows isn't even his name, Isabella." He's looking at me over the frame of his glasses now, his brown eyes staring deep into my soul.

They look as worn out as I feel. I've given everything to this paper the almost four years I've been at this school. I'm in my final semester. This right here? It feels like a huge betrayal. Like everything I've held close to me, all the pieces of my soul that were wrapped in this have been completely shattered; scattered against the ground like glass shards.

"What *is* his name then, Pete?" I speak to him in the same tone he used to speak to me.

He sighs deeply, looking at me pointedly. "You're lucky we were friends before I became your professor. No one else would put up with this attitude."

"It isn't an attitude. I'm asking you a legit question. What's his real name?"

"That's one of the things you'll learn in the interview." He leans back in his chair, steepling his fingers together. "You've coasted through the past almost-four years here, and it's time for you to show me what you're made of."

My stomach drops. I'm here on a scholarship, the first in my family to get more than a fucking GED. I'll hold onto my future with my nails digging trenches into the dirt. Tilting my head to the side, I shoot him a death glare. I haven't coasted in any type of way. I've paid my dues, done everything each editor of this paper before me has done. "So you're threatening me with my degree? Need I remind you of all the accomplishments we've received while I've been editor-in-chief?"

"Let's be honest with one another. Most of those accomplishments had the groundwork laid before you showed up. You and I both know all you had to do was keep the status quo. You brought nothing new to the table. What I'm telling you is that if you want to graduate with your Bachelor's in Communications, you need to prove to me you can do the hard work - even if this particular story isn't considered hard work for you."

"It's not considered a sport to me," I argue. "And that's not what I'm going into Journalism for, Pete. I don't have this great dream to write about the next MMA or whatever star he is. We both know he does whatever fight comes to him, seems to me he has an anger issue that's unchecked."

"It's human interest, Isabella. Who's to say you'll be able to get the job you want? When you're out there in the big, bad world, things aren't always what they seem. What if the only job available is at the local newspaper for the sports section? Will you tell them no? How will you live? And all of us in this business know that word gets around. If you give up more than one job, you won't get offers anymore. You know it's true."

A part of me wants to say I would tell them no. I would keep my pride and refuse to do things that compromise my belief system. There's a stubbornness in my mind that wants to argue I'd be the exception rather than the rule. At the same time, I know I must eat, and my parents will expect me to pay my own bills once I graduate. They've floated me while I've been here, and they've been more than clear that once I have that piece of paper in my hand, it's all on me. Especially since I realize how hard it is for them to help. My mom tells me every time I talk to her. What he's saying does make sense, even though I hate to admit it. "Are you setting up the interview for me?"

He chuckles before taking a drink of his water. "Negative. You're going to do this all on your own, from contacting him, to securing the interview. I'm wishing you luck though, because in the seven years I've known him, he's never given an interview. He'd prefer to not speak, rather than. It's going to take a miracle to get him to talk to you in the first place."

"I feel like you're setting me up for failure, and I don't appreciate it." I'm beginning to think the worst. It's hard knowing everything is stacked against me. The only situation I've been in like this before is trying to figure out how to make college work. This one is uncomfortable.

"Failure isn't an option, Isabella. Any work you've done previous to this doesn't matter, it won't even count. Your entire grade rides on what you do in this moment."

He drops another fucking bomb. This one I really hadn't expected.

"That's not fair," I whisper, trying to push the heaviness out of my chest and the tightness out of my throat. Every single thing I've worked for is disappearing right before my eyes.

Pete levels me with his gaze. "Life isn't fair, and as soon as you realize that, the better off you'll be. This isn't an easy job. Why do you think I'm a professor at a college instead of off in the warzone? As humans we do what we have to in order to survive, and I'm telling you, this is what you must do."

I sigh heavily, finally facing and understanding the obstacles he's laying down in front of me. "Just so you know, I resent you for this."

"It's okay if you resent me," he drops his pen on his desk, folding his hands in front of his chin. "I'm trying to get you prepared for reality, something I wish others had done when I was in your shoes. You understand?"

"Yeah," I glare as I cross my arms over my chest. "I guess I get you're trying to make me a better person and a good journalist, but this feels like a personal attack. I have to be honest with you."

"You gonna be able to do it?"

"Is there really an option that I don't?" I question, giving him a look of death, wishing with everything I have that it would cause him to expire right on the spot. "I've not gone to school for four years to get this damned close to have you pull it away from me."

"I'm not pulling it away from you; *you'll* be pulling it away."

Inside I'm fuming, ready to stop right now and give up everything I've worked for, but I have to keep my cool. My family sacrificed a lot to get me here. Hell, I did too. The long night studying to get the scholarship that's helped pay for a good portion of my education. If I don't finish the degree, or fail, I could be forced to pay back what's been given to me. Pete knows all of this as a friend, and my freshman advisor. "How long do I have to accomplish this?"

"Six weeks, from start to finish."

"Six weeks?!" I parrot back at him, feeling that pit in my stomach increase into a damn crater.

"I didn't stutter, right? There are seven weeks until this semester is over, and you need to have everything turned in to me with enough time for me to grade it."

"But we have this semester and next before I graduate. I've known you long enough to know you typically grade both of them together. I feel like you've decided to fuck me over, *Professor*." Any other teacher I wouldn't say those words to, but this one? He knows me better than anyone else. He knows my dreams and what I want to accomplish. It's almost as if it's impossible.

"You tell me you don't think you're up to it, I'll fail you right now. You can do this, Isabella. Don't disappoint me."

If there's anything I hate, it's someone telling me I'll fail. I've worked hard to be where I am in life, and I'll be damned if I let anything stand in my way. Not to mention pulling the disappointment card was a low fucking blow. "I'm up to it. I'll give you the best interview you've ever read in your life."

"I'm expecting that from you. Go out there and get it."

He turns away from me, and I know at this moment I'm dismissed. Grabbing my purse and bag, I shoulder them both before getting up and leaving the office. It's taken everything I have to hold my shit together, but no more.

Once I'm outside, I let my cheeks heat and the flush of anger flow over my body. This is the stuff I do my best to keep in, to not allow others to see, but dammit, I'm pissed right now.

It's a long haul down the hill to student parking. If I

thought I could make it without falling on my face, I'd take off at a run and get rid of all these feelings inside my chest. But I haven't run in at least two years, and I don't want anyone having to call the ambulance on me because I've about killed myself. When I see my SUV, I pick up the pace, ready to get inside so I can let loose with the tears clogging up my throat. Beeping the doors, I fumble, opening the driver's side as quickly as I can. Tossing my bag and purse in the passenger seat, I crank the heat and rest my forehead against the steering wheel, finally letting the tears fall.

Purchase Now

Shadows

RENEGADE
WHITNEY

LATE MARCH

"Ryan, I'm tellin' you, I need my hair pulled, a red hand-print across my ass, someone licking my nipples, a dick in my treasure cove. I need it all."

Drunk. I am drunk. Like way past the legal limit – otherwise I wouldn't be sitting here spilling all my secrets to my baby brother's best friend. The baby brother who had been totally unplanned by my parents. Ten years my junior, baby brother. He and Ryan are the same age; twenty-five to my thirty-five. Makes me feel so much older just thinking about it. Not only by age, but by life experience, too, although they've probably got me beat. They're cops and have served overseas in the military. Dear Lord, I think I sound like Julia Sugarbaker from Designing Women. I'm three sheets to the wind, and nobody stopped me.

I see him try to suppress a grin as he brings his beer up to his lips, taking a nice long pull off the wide mouth. I am mesmerized by the way his throat muscles move when he swallows, pushing the liquid down his throat. No denying he's all man. None of the boyhood shyness he always had with me is anywhere near us tonight. The palm of his hand completely covers the label, the one drink he takes drains half the bottle. For a second he focuses on my face, squinting as he watches me. "How many of those have you had to drink?" He points the neck of his beer to the wine glass in my hand.

His voice is as smooth as the red liquid I swirl in my glass. I tilt my head to the side, realizing the whole room goes right along with it. Counting back, I try to think how many I had before he took the seat next to mine, and I can't remember. "Five or six?" I ask him, like he should know. "What's it to you, Ren-e-gade," I sound out his name by syllables. My words sound slightly slurred to my own ears. "Renegade," I grin. "Anybody ever tell you, you little boys and your nicknames are cute? Just like playing cops and robbers...you with your Renegade, Trevor with his Tank," I'm giggling for real now. "Pew, pew!" I fake shoot him with my finger gun, thinking how pissed off my brother would be if he were here right now. Not Ryan, though, he's patient. God bless him.

"You think maybe it's time you quit for the night?" He gently moves to take what I have left away from me.

His fingers are soft as they try to pry mine from around the stem, but I resist his attempts and pull it closer to my chest. The liquid sloshes and I inhale deeply, hoping not to lose any of it. I'm like a two-year-old with my blankie. This glass of wine is my security and at this moment I'll protect it with everything I have. Once the security is gone, I'm left with nothing. I can't be transparent tonight, I need something shielding me from my reality. I'm a woman on the prowl, and a woman on the prowl is confident in her abilities.

"Quit?" I ask, running my tongue over my dry lips, trying to moisten them so I can form words more easily. "Quitting is not something I do. That's what my ex-husband did. My mama did.

That's what my former boss did," I shake my head and try to stand on four-inch stilettos. He reaches out and grabs my elbow, steadying me, being a rock when I haven't had one in a very long time. "Whitney Trumbolt is not a fuckin' quitter." I make my voice as strong and as clear as possible, I fear though that it comes out a slurred mess.

I can see Ryan try again to keep the smile from his face. The corners of his lips twitch, and it pisses me off. Not because I'm mad, but because he thinks it's funny. He thinks this is a joke, and it's not. It's my life. The life I've been trying so desperately to get out from under or save. I'm not sure which yet. All I know is I haven't been living and I'm damn sick of the in-between.

"You think this is funny?" I take another drink from my wine glass. It's a big one this time, I drain it. There's not one drop left when I set it back down on the bar, slapping my lips together with a satisfied pop.

"No, Whit, I think you're having a bad night." His tone is one someone would use with a kindergartner, talking them down from a temper tantrum. It pisses me off too.

A bad night? Try a bad decade. If I could do anything, it would go back to the night I turned twenty-five and be the age that Ryan is again. I would do so many things differently, I would change so much about the choices I made back then. "You know nothing about me, other than the fact that I'm Tank's older sister."

He grabs me by the wrist, locking his hand around the flesh. I feel his fingers lightly touch the skin and bone. It's more of a caress than a warning. I never realized until this moment how much bigger he is than me. Never really paid any kind of attention to it – oh I've paid attention to him off and on through-out the years, but never like this.

Ryan "Renegade" Kepler rises to his full height, towering

over me as I do my best to keep my footing and ignore the way my skin tingles where he grips my wrist. He leans in close – so close I can feel his breath on my skin.

"I know a lot of things about you that you don't think I know."

His voice is hard and soft at the same time. I close my eyes to savor it, to try and figure out how he's able to do both. Maybe it's my drunken mind, but he's magic to me in this instant. The deep timbre rushes over me as I try to understand his words, but I'm having a hard time. This is the closest I've been to a man in a very long time. My body is at attention, as is my libido. I press my thighs together as I dig my heels in deeper, not because I don't want him to move me, because I ache. It's an ache that's never been fulfilled, if I'm honest.

"I know that you love your mama's fried chicken, your grandmother's homemade mac and cheese, Alabama football, and Dale Earnhardt Jr. I know that you have a soft heart. Hallmark movies make you cry, you pick up strays on the side of the road, and you always buy that homeless man near the Starbucks a morning coffee," he lulls me into a sense of security. Making me want to believe there is someone out there who listens when I talk, someone who looks at me and sees a brain behind my blonde hair.

I'm wrapped up in his voice, in the things he does know about me. Things I never knew he paid attention to. I'm swaying, but it's because his voice is doing weird things to my equilibrium. His other hand cups my hip and I can feel the heat of his body through the material of my skirt. My thighs burn as they're pressed against his where we stand.

"I know that your ex-husband was a piece of shit. I know that your ex-boss didn't know what the hell to do with the creative genius that is your mind, and I know that your mama will never forgive you for giving up pageants, but she'll never forgive herself for pushing you that damn hard," he stops and pulls back, giving me his eyes and face to stare at.

Our eyes meet – his brown to my blue – and I realize with clarity that I'm breathing hard, hard enough that it feels as if I've run a marathon. The loss of his strong body against mine makes me want to cry. I want to grasp at his clothing, pull him back in, and let him heat up parts of me that have been cold for so long.

"You wanna know what else I know?" The question is asked in a way that says he's not sure if he wants an answer. The way his face closes off and he withdraws slightly into himself make me think this is a secret he's not shared with anyone. Tonight, I want him to share it with me; I want to be the person he confides in. He knows so much about me, I want to know everything about him too. There's a string of awareness stretched between us, and it's pulling me closer.

I'm captivated by the way the dim lights of the bar make his brown eyes darker, I'm enthralled by the fact that it looks like it's been a few days since he shaved, and I'm even more fascinated by the cut he has on his cheek. He and Tank went out on a call last night, and I can't help but wonder if that cut is the result of a dangerous night doing a dangerous job.

I shake my head and then nod, because I'm conflicted in my drunkenness, but I do want to find out what else he knows. I step forward, put my arms around his neck, and lean up so that now I'm the one in his ear. The truth of the matter is I need to feel close to him, I want the heat back he's taken away from me. I'm cold without it, and I'm sick to death of being cold. "Tell me what else you know."

I see him look around the bar, checking to make sure that we're not being paid any attention to. He bends with his knees and grips my ass cheeks in the palms of his hands, bringing us flush together so our bodies touch. His voice is dark as he all but growls. "I know I'm the one who can put my dick in that treasure cove. I know I'm the one that can pull that hair, I can pull on those nipples, and I can smack this ass," he squeezes my flesh like he owns it, where his hands rest. "The question is – will you let me?"

It's not a question I can say *no* to. The way the air crackles between us, the alcohol I've consumed, and the sudden fascination I have with his heat. There's not any way that I can say no nor is there any desire on my part to deny it. I've denied myself a lot of things in this life and this right here is not something that I want to brush off. This is God giving me what I want on a silver platter, a sacrificial offering for the shit I've gone through the past few years. This is my Cinderella moment and my SEC Championship all tied together into one great big bow. Over six feet and two hundred pounds of bow. If I say no, Lord, never offer me anything else because I'm gonna be a nun for the rest of my life.

"You're what?" He asks, a glimmer of surprise and playfulness in his eyes.

I said that out loud? Never mind, I can fix this.

"Yes," I breathe out, adding on a "please."

"Oh baby, you don't have to beg. I'll do whatever you need me to," Ryan says as I find my hand in his and stumble to keep up as he pulls us out of the bar. We pass people we've known our whole lives, clients I've helped to the altar, and I'm pretty sure we just passed the Deacon of the church. No one stops us as we hit the front door. I gulp in the fresh air, sure as the world my senses are going to come to me.

Guess what? They don't. I'm in for whatever this full moon-lit night is going to bring us. Safe Whitney is not putting the brakes on a ride crazier than a lap at Talladega. No, Wild Whitney has taken her place. Funny how both are four letter words, yet they couldn't be further apart.

In mere minutes I'm in his truck, and we're headed towards my house. I will myself not to pass out, because for the first time in years, I want to be here and present for this experience that's about to happen. I want to remember every damn detail. If it's only going to be for this one night, I don't want to miss a thing.

Download Below

Renegade

ONLY THE BEGINNING

THE CROWD SCREAMED LOUDLY, causing her palms to sweat and her heart to race. Harmony Stewart inhaled deeply and then exhaled, letting the breath flow through her. The relaxation technique worked. Shoulders that had been so tight she couldn't even roll them were now loose. It was always like this, she realized. Right before she went on stage, the nervous energy started, causing her to tense up—not fully being able to appreciate the life she was living. Closing her eyes, she breathed again, feeling her muscles loosen up even more.

"Harmony, you're up next."

She nodded, glancing at the production tech. "Thanks." Her voice was thin even to her own ears. This was just something that she went through, no matter how many millions of albums she sold or awards she garnered.

Looking out onto the stage, she saw the rock group, Black Friday, finishing up. A fan of the band, she tried to still the heart that threatened to beat out of her chest as they finished their song and walked towards her. The lead singer was the personification of hotness in her opinion. She had always wanted a meeting, but had never been able to approach him when they had been in the same space. This time he would have to walk right by her—not that she had deluded herself to think he would know who she even was. Pulling her shaking hands to her body, she gripped them hard as the group approached.

"Good job, guys," she smiled as they passed her. One by one, they nodded and accepted her smile until she came face to face with Reaper, the lead singer. She only knew his stage name. What she wouldn't give to know his real one.

"Thanks. Good luck out there, sweetheart," he smiled widely. His teeth were white and straight, the dimples that she had caught glimpses of in pictures deepened widely in his cheeks. He was tall, much taller than she had originally thought. He towered over her 5'6 frame (with heels, thank you very much), and the tattoos that traveled down his arms were a feast to her eyes. They were intricate, and she wished she had the time to study them all.

Harmony opened her mouth to tell him something else, but he was already gone. Disappointment hit her stomach hard and fast. But at least it had been a start. With any luck, she would see him at some other award show. She heard her cue as she looked back to where the rock band stood, debriefing with some of their management. For just a split second, her eyes met Reaper's and goose bumps appeared on her arms. If only they'd had more time.

———

REAPER SAT with his head back, eyes closed. The night had been long. He never really liked doing these awards shows, but their fans were amazing. Even though they didn't have what others called "crossover" success, they had some of the most rabid fans in the music industry. That, however, didn't change the fact that he was lonely and tired of not having someone besides the members of his band to share his life with.

"Who was the cutie that smiled at us as we walked by?"

"That was Harmony Stewart," he answered, moving only his lips.

"Country singer?"

"Yes, dude," he sighed. "The country singer."

"She's cuter than I imagined. I've only seen her on TV a few times."

Reaper sighed again. "Seriously Train, you're getting on my fuckin' nerves. Do you have to talk all the time?"

"What's your problem? Do you need to get laid?" Train asked, having a seat next to his friend.

"Do you ever get sick of all this?" He lifted his long arms and big hands up; gesturing to the backstage green room they sat in.

"Sick of what? The free pussy, the free booze, the amazing trips overseas and around this great nation? Playing the music we love every night? I'm ready to do this the rest of my life. Why aren't you?"

Reaper lifted his head up and opened his eyes, staring into the eyes of his friend. "I'm burnt out. Not with the music, but with the lifestyle. I need a change, something different to shake things up."

"Burnt out? How can you be burnt out?"

"It's just..." he ran his fingers through his hair. "We've been on the road for a year. I need something new and exciting in my life. I'm sick of the same girls, the same bus, and the same hotel rooms."

"You're bein' a moody fucking pansy is what you're being. Do you know how many guys would give their left nut to be where we are?" Train slapped his friend on the shoulder, the disbelief showing on his face.

Reaper realized he would get nowhere with his friend. Train dealt with his demons in unhealthy ways and perhaps tonight wasn't the best time to approach him about this. He couldn't rightfully explain his feelings if he didn't fully understand them himself. Better to just pretend that everything was peachy. "You're right. I'm crazy. I just need some good alcohol and a good cigarette. Let's get to the after party."

"Now that's what I'm talkin' about," the lead guitarist said, grabbing his friend by the arm and ushering him out of the room.

Reaper realized that nobody seemed to care what he thought, how he felt, or just how lonely he was. He might as well make the best of what to him was an unbearable situation.

"HARMONY? Are you changing into the dress that new designer sent you for the after party?"

"I think so," Harmony answered her best friend and assistant, Shell.

"You need to change now, then."

Harmony rolled her eyes and grabbed the hanger from Shell's hand. "Yes ma'am."

Used to bossing her friend around, Shell had a seat while Harmony changed. "So tell me, did you meet anybody interesting at this awards show?"

"I did. Did you see any of the show?"

"I didn't get a chance too, no. I wish I had, but there was a lot going on back here," Shell answered from behind the door that Harmony had closed to change.

"I'm so sorry, Shell. I know how hard you work, and you'll

never fully know how much I appreciate it. You'll be excited to hear that I finally met the guys from Black Friday."

Harmony heard the squeal and couldn't help the smile that spread across her face.

"I am so damn jealous. That lead singer—was he as hot as he looks on TV?"

"Even more so. I actually said a few words to him. Top moment of my life this year—for real."

She finished changing and let herself out of the dressing room. Coming out, she turned around in a circle, making sure everything looked okay. For the show, Harmony had wanted to keep it classy and her dress had been very Old Hollywood. This dress, however, was young and fun. Sparkles and glitter reigned. The hot pink color showed off the tan she had been able to get during a short vacation before awards season ramped up.

"Does this look okay?" she asked, turning around again so Shell could see her from every angle.

"You look really good. Hoping to meet anybody at this party?"

"You never know," she shrugged. "Maybe the guys from Black Friday will be there, and I'll be able to say something else to them. I was kind of a blabbering fool earlier. Are you coming with me?"

Shell wrinkled her nose up at her friend. "I don't know. This hasn't been a stellar day for me."

"All the more reason for you to raid my closet, find something hot, and come out on the town with me."

"Why are you trying to corrupt me? Usually it's the other way around. You're the belle of the country ball, and I'm the one trying to get you to do Jager shots," Shell laughed.

"Maybe I'm ready to let my hair down. It's time. I am twenty-four years old, and I'm not gettin' any younger. If I keep goin' at this pace with the music, I'm not goin' to be married before thirty, and that's never who I wanted to be. I'm the type of girl who wants a boyfriend, wants to be in love. I'm gonna have to make that a priority."

Shell knew that Harmony was telling the truth. She was one of those women who were made to be in love, but she wasn't for sure that her friend had ever felt those feelings. Her one serious relationship hadn't ended well and left her feeling disconnected. It was nice to see that she was beginning to look past that time in her life. "Okay, okay. If I need to be there to keep you from asking the first man you meet to marry you, I'll be there to save you from yourself."

"You, Shell, are the best friend a girl could ask for." She reached over, kissing her on the cheek.

"YOU SURE WE can leave in an hour?" Reaper asked as he unfolded himself from the backseat of the limo they had taken to the party location.

"Yes, I'm sure," Train answered with a huff. Reaper didn't miss the way he wiped the back of his hand over his nose. It was a sure sign that some things never changed. He raised his eyebrows as Train admonished him. "Dude, when did you become such a fucking killjoy?"

"I told you already, I'm just not feeling this tonight."

They got into line with the rest of the celebrities and the other members of their band to walk the red carpet that lead into the venue that housed the party for the night.

"Hey." Train hit his friend's elbow. "Isn't that the little country girl from earlier?" He pointed further up the carpet.

Reaper couldn't see for shit, so he squinted his eyes together, trying to bring the person in front of them better in focus. "Fuck," he mumbled, pulling the wrap-around sunglasses he normally wore on stage up to his eyes. They were part of his persona, but in actuality they were prescription and without them—he really couldn't see. "Yeah, that's her."

"Cute, isn't she?"

"Seriously man, we already talked about how cute she is."

At that moment, they walked onto the main part of the carpet. Flashbulbs went off as they plastered smiles on their faces. Photographers called their names from all around. A little further down the aisle a photographer yelled at Reaper.

"What sweetheart? Didn't hear you." He cupped his hand over his ear.

"Take a picture with Harmony. It'll be a good photo op."

Harmony heard the exchange from where she stood and laughed. "He might not want to be seen with someone like me," she smiled as she glanced back at him.

He couldn't tell if she was flirting with him or not, but he figured he would seize the day. "Nah, darlin' maybe you don't wanna be seen with someone like me."

A blush covered her face, and she turned around so that she faced him. "I'm a fan, seriously. I'd love to take a picture with you."

The smile she gave him made his stomach dance. He had faced huge crowds before overseas. Hundreds of thousands of people he had performed in front of and not been nervous. Approaching this woman with the smile on her face made his legs shake. He strode over to her and easily put his arm around her waist. Even wearing heels she only came up to his shoulder.

"Where do you want us to look?" he asked.

The amount of people screaming at them was so deafening neither one of them could understand what anyone was saying. "Let's just start looking to the left and then look to the right," she said as she gripped his waist.

They stood there for long minutes as everyone got their pictures—and when it was over, the two of them were reluctant to let go of each other.

"Thanks Reaper and Harmony," the original photographer told them.

"You're welcome," Harmony answered. She pulled her arm from around his waist and turned to face him. "Thanks for taking a picture with me. I guess I'll see you inside and maybe, just maybe, I'll learn what people call you besides Reaper?"

"If I tell you that, then I'd have to kill you. It's highly classified." He put his hands in the pockets of the pants he wore and rocked back on his heels.

She wasn't sure if he was flirting with her or not because she couldn't see his eyes, but she knew that they were staring right at her. "Well then, I guess I better figure out how to work on my security clearance." She gave him a flip of her hair as she turned from him and walked towards the entrance of the club.

The pictures were already making their way all over the world.

Download Below

Only The Beginning

ALSO BY LARAMIE BRISCOE

The Haldonia Monarchy

Royal Rebel

Heaven Hill Series

Meant To Be

Out of Darkness

Losing Control

Worth The Battle

Dirty Little Secret

Second Chance Love

Rough Patch

Beginning of Forever

Home Free

Shield My Heart

A Heaven Hill Christmas

Heaven Hill Next Generation

Hurricane

Wild

Fury

Hollow

Restraint

Bishop

Heaven Hill Shorts

Caelin

Christine

Justice

Harley

Jagger

Charity

Liam

Drew

Dalton

Mandy

Rockin' Country Series

Only The Beginning

The Price of Love

Full Circle

Hard To Love

Reaper's Love

The Nashvegas Trilogy

Power Couple

Breach of Contract

Platinum

The Moonshine Task Force Series

Renegade

Tank

Havoc

Ace

Menace

Cruise

Laurel Springs Emergency Response Team

Ransom

Suppression

Enigma

Cutter

Sullivan

Devante

Archer

The MVP Duet

On the DL

MVP

The Midnight Cove Series

Inflame

Stand Alones

Shadows

Sketch

Sass

Trick

Room 143

2018 Laramie Briscoe Compilation

2019 Laramie Briscoe Compilation

ABOUT THE AUTHOR

Laramie Briscoe is the USA Today and Wall Street Journal Bestselling Author of over 30 books.

Since self-publishing her first book in May of 2013, Laramie has appeared on the Top 100 Bestselling E-books Lists on Amazon Kindle, Apple Books, Barnes & Noble, and Kobo. Her books have been known to make readers laugh and cry. They are guaranteed to be emotional, steamy reads.

When she's not writing alpha males who seriously love their women, she loves spending time with friends, reading, and marathoning shows on Netflix. Married to her high school sweetheart, Laramie lives in Bowling Green, KY with her husband (the Travel Coordinator) and an energetic Pudel-pointer, Gus.

facebook.com/authorlaramiebriscoe

twitter.com/laramiebriscoe

instagram.com/laramie_briscoe

bookbub.com/authors/laramie-briscoe

REPORT ERRORS/REVIEWS

LEAVE A REVIEW

IF THERE WAS a part you loved of "Declan", please don't hesitate to leave a review and let other readers know!

If you do leave a review, please email me with the link so that I can say a personal 'thank you'!!! They mean a lot, and I want to let you know I appreciate you taking the time out of your day!

Email Me

REPORT AN ERROR

Also, if you find an error, know that it has slipped through no less than four sets of eyes, and it is a mistake. Please let me know, if you find one, and if I agree it's an error. It will be changed. Thank you!

Report Errors

CONNECT WITH LARAMIE

Patreon:
patreon.com/laramiebriscoe
Website:
www.laramiebriscoe.net
Facebook:
facebook.com/AuthorLaramieBriscoe
Twitter:
twitter.com/LaramieBriscoe
Pinterest:
pinterest.com/laramiebriscoe
Instagram:
instagram.com/laramie_briscoe
Mailing List:
http://sitel.ink/LBList
Email:
laramie@laramiebriscoe.com

Made in the USA
Las Vegas, NV
16 March 2024

87306543R00121